YOU [illegible] A HORSE TO MURDER

A Secrets of Sanctuary Cozy Mystery

Book #1

TARA MEYERS

ISBN-13: 978-1985448230
ISBN-10: 1985448238

You Can Lead a Horse to Murder

Forest Grove Books
Editor Christina Schrunk

AUTHOR'S NOTE

I've been writing a middle grade mystery series for several years now, The Samantha Wolf Mysteries, and it was a natural transition to move into cozies. (You can find those titles under my pen name, Tara Ellis) I'm a firm believer in delivering an intriguing story with likeable characters the reader can relate to. I chose to place it all in a welcoming setting that leaves you wishing you could visit there. While I enjoy a suspenseful story, I also prefer to immerse myself in one that leaves me with a good feeling at the end. My goal is to achieve this with the Secrets of Sanctuary series, and I hope you love Ember Burns as much as I do!

BOOKS BY TARA MEYERS

Find these titles on her Amazon author page!

The Chris Echo Files

A Distant Echo (a short story)
Echo of Fear

Secrets of Sanctuary Cozy Mysteries

You Can Lead a Horse to Murder
Man's Best Alibi (Coming this Spring!)
Cat's Got Your Arsenic (TBA)

If you have enjoyed these books, you might want to check out her other titles written as Amazon bestselling author, Tara Ellis. These include a fun middle grade mystery series, a young adult science fiction trilogy, and a true stories of survival series!

ONE

The small mountain town of Sanctuary, Washington, had a way of luring you in and never letting go.

Ember Burns slammed the tailgate of her truck before leaning warily against it. There was no denying the beauty of the valley they were nestled in, and she paused for a moment to appreciate it. The jagged outline of the Cascade Mountains cast a long shadow before the rising sun. Tumbling hillsides were draped in evergreens that spilled out into the valley, blanketing it with the woods Ember came to know as a child. Closing her eyes, she envisioned the solace of those woods and the smell of the fallen pine needles warmed in the summer heat. Letting out a slow breath, she looked again to the top of the peak and, feeling the power of the landscape, was ready to press on.

It had been a long week. A long month, really.

That was when she'd come back to Sanctuary to say goodbye to her mom forever. It was a beautiful ceremony on another gorgeous summer afternoon, but it was the darkest day of Ember's life.

Pushing the gloomy thought aside, she forced a smile before looking up at the rustic sign she'd just finished hanging. Tilting her head first one way and then the other, Ember squinted and pursed her lips. It looked crooked.

I should have let Blaine help me hang it! Kicking half-heartedly at one of the trucks balding tires, she walked out into the street to examine the storefront from a distance.

"Sanctuary Animal Clinic," she read aloud. Not very original, but it got the message across. Glancing at the neighboring stores, she confirmed that the styling matched the quaint southwestern theme of the town.

Banners were strung across the narrow street at every intersection, advertising the upcoming centennial celebration on the Fourth of July. Originally a logging town set deep in the mountains of Washington State, Sanctuary now relied primarily on farming and tourism for its income.

When Ember left ten years ago for college, a young eighteen-year-old ready to take on the world, she didn't think she'd live there again. But plans changed.

A fresh wave of guilt built in her chest, forcing her to place a hand over her racing heart. The anxiety started the day of the funeral and wasn't letting up. She'd need to go for a hike soon. It was one of the ways she re-centered herself.

Slipping a scrunchie from her wrist, Ember gathered her long red hair into a ponytail with practiced ease. She still had a lot of work to do. The best way to keep her mind off her mother's sudden passing was to stay busy. Walking back to her truck, she caught her reflection in the large storefront window of her clinic.

Pausing, Ember looked first at the shadowy towering mountains behind her before studying her image. Of average height and build, her most conspicuous feature was her crimson-red hair. As a child, it was her greatest source of torment. That and her green eyes were the genetic contribution of her Scottish father, but she had a bronzed complexion, thanks to her mom's Lakota lineage.

Ember never quite forgave her parents for her name. She was already doomed to being the butt of all the jokes at school because of her red hair, but combined with the name Ember *Burns*, it was enough to make even her teachers chuckle.

It wasn't until she was around seventeen or eighteen that, somehow, a miracle transpired, and suddenly, her radiant locks became a cause for envy rather than torture. Ember now embraced her unique appearance, but if it weren't for being the last to carry the Burns name, she would have legally changed it.

I think Dr. Flame would look better on a business card, she mused, causing herself to chuckle. Giving her ponytail a shake, she turned away and went to rummage in the tool chest in the bed of her truck. The hammer she'd just used had somehow disappeared. Both the vehicle and its contents were her mom's. Ember's small sedan was safely tucked away in the garage back at the family home. It got great gas mileage but was useless for moving things around, and that was all she'd been doing for the past two weeks. First, her belongings into the family home, and now office furniture at the clinic.

Everything happened in a whirlwind of activity the month before. The day after her mom was laid to rest, Ember was presented with a will which left her the modest farmhouse and twenty acres on a lake at the edge of town. It also left her a reasonable amount of money from a life insurance policy Ember had known nothing about.

It was an accidental death. Well, that's what the law ruled it, but Ember felt the man who chose to drive drunk that night didn't do so accidentally.

Finding and grabbing the elusive hammer, she reorganized the displaced items in the tool chest. Her father died when she was just a baby, so she was now officially an orphan at the age of 28. Gripping the hammer tight enough to turn her knuckles white, Ember looked up again at the sign, blinking rapidly to prevent any fresh tears from spilling. It was time to move forward, and she was excited to be doing it at home, in Sanctuary. But there was still a lot to do, and she wanted to make her mom proud.

Between the life and auto insurance policies, she was able to pay for the funeral, pay off the rest of her student loans, and still have enough to live off of for some time. The house was paid for, but there was plenty of upkeep involved. She could have sold it and returned to her internship. She was about to start her third year at a prestigious animal hospital where she'd already gotten the large animal endorsement to her DVM—Doctor of Veterinary Medicine.

Instead, she'd made an impulsive purchase, thanks in part to her Aunt Becky. She had set Ember up for a lunch date with Dr. Bernie Chambers, the only veterinarian in Sanctuary for over forty years. He'd closed down his practice earlier that year and was flying out to Florida to a 65-and-over community the next day. He threw out a figure for the building and most of its contents that Ember was unable to resist.

Somehow, in the few days she'd been led back home, she'd been sucked in without even realizing it. Sitting there with a literal offer on the table, she found she didn't want to leave. Everything she wanted was right there, and the fresh loss of her mom was softened by a sense of hope and adventure for something new.

A month later, her life had completely changed. Now that she was committed, she was determined to be successful. Financially, she figured she had enough to float the business for six months. Being handed a forty-year-old client list should help make the transition a little smoother. At least, that was what Ember was banking on.

"Your sign is crooked."

Spinning around, Ember shaded her eyes against the glare of the sun and spotted her Aunt Becky leaning out the window of her SUV.

"Thanks for the tip." Giving a mock salute, Ember lowered the tailgate back down and climbed onto it. Prying the nail out, she turned to look back at Becky. "Here?" she asked, raising the sign about an inch.

"Perfect!" Becky shouted before pulling into the parking space next to Ember's rusty pickup. Climbing out, she batted at some stray strands of red hair a shade lighter than Ember's and then rested her hands on her hips. "Blaine did a good job on the woodwork."

After sinking the nail back in and repositioning the sign, Ember jumped down next to her aunt. "Yeah, thanks for the referral. He got it done fast."

"Did he hit on you? I hope you took my advice and turned him down."

"Yeah, he hit on me," Ember confirmed, laughing. "And don't worry. I broke his heart, even though it meant having to hang a crooked sign by myself."

Wagging a finger as she walked around and opened the passenger door, the older woman's expression grew serious. "The last thing you need right now is a man thrown into the mix. You have enough to worry about."

Becky's fourteen-year-old daughter emerged from the vehicle, rolling her eyes at her mother's dramatics. "Blaine is kinda cute in an old man sort of way."

"Old man?" Ember chortled. "He's not even thirty! Gosh, Beck, when did Elizabeth grow up, and how did I already cross into the 'old' category?"

"Get used to it," Becky retorted without humor. "I'm barely past forty, and you'd think I was born in the middle ages, listening to this menagerie talk."

Right on cue, two ten-year-old boys literally fell from the back seat, squawking as a large, cinnamon-colored labradoodle bulled through them.

While Elizabeth had dark hair and eyes, the twin boys were blessed with the Burns family's red hair. Becky was Ember's dad's younger sister by twelve years. When he died, she became close friends with Ember's mom and, as a result, was more like an older sister to her while growing up.

"Who's your newest rescue?" Ember asked, nodding at the dog now running in circles around the laughing boys. Opening the front door, she motioned for the group to follow her inside the clinic.

"Ummm … Bret and Tim named her Cujo." Becky made a grab for the dog but missed, having to settle for a hand on a shoulder of each of her sons. "Stop running! You're getting her too worked up."

"Aside from the obvious fact that Cujo is a boy's name, it's totally unoriginal." Ember took a dog treat from a dish on the front counter and tossed it to

Cujo. While she was updating most of the old rundown furniture, the main counter and all of the stocked products were staying.

"Feel free to change it."

She glanced at her aunt and then paused when she saw the smile on her face.

"Uh-uh," Ember insisted, crossing her arms over chest. Becky Stratton ran an animal shelter and headed a rescue program. There was only one reason she would bring a dog to Ember that wasn't properly named. "You said it yourself; I have too much on my plate. A dog is the *last* thing I need!"

"I've already got four dogs," Becky quipped. "And three cats."

"Becky …"

"And two horses, a goat, and a couple of pigs."

"Aunt Becky!"

"What? We've also just inherited a new chicken to our already impressive flock, which the bunnies don't seem to like much."

"I can't take in a dog right now."

"Did I mention the guinea pig? It drives the parakeet crazy. It's trying to mimic the small little squeaks and clicks it makes, but it can't quite get it right."

"I think it sounds *just* like it," Bret offered, nodding. "Oh, I forgot to tell you that Cujo got out again."

Eyes widening, Becky looked at her son with disdain.

"I thought *she* was Cujo," Ember questioned, gesturing to the dog.

As if knowing she was being talked about, "Cujo" sat down next to Ember and stared at her silently.

"No, the *real* Cujo," Tim corrected. "Bret's gerbil. He likes to bite."

"And escape his cage," Becky added. "The last time it happened, it took almost a week to get him back, and how many bites?"

Bret wiggled under his mother's scrutiny. "I *swear* I latched the cover!"

"I'm putting out a rat trap!" Elizabeth declared. "If that thing comes in my room, he's a goner!"

"Mom!" Bret demanded, stomping a foot. "Tell Lizzy she can't kill Cujo!"

Turning from her kids, Becky looked at Ember and spread her arms wide. "Would you really banish this poor soul to the unknown fate of a killer gerbil on the loose?"

Laughing, Ember knelt down next to the lab-and-poodle mix. She was a medium-sized dog of around fifty pounds. Her curly hair was a gorgeous hue of red, a few shades lighter than her own. Looking into the warm chocolate-brown eyes, she was struck by a sense of intelligence and understanding.

"Where did she come from? You know how expensive labradoodles are, and she looks purebred."

Grinning, Becky winked conspiratorially at her kids before kneeling down on the other side of the dog. She knew she had her.

"Sort of a strange thing. She was found out in a field off Hwy 12, about ten miles out, dirty and hungry without a collar. I scanned for a chip, of course, but she doesn't have one. Contacted all the other neighboring shelters, and no one seems to be looking for her." Shrugging, she rubbed the dog affectionately. "Kept her quarantined at the shelter for a week, and I've had her out at our place for about ten days now. Nothing. No inquires, no answers to my ad. It's time to place her in a forever home, Ember, and she's a special one. I really would keep her myself, but I think she'd be better off with you."

"And why is that?"

"Because I know you'll love her in a way she deserves. Plus, she'd make a good watch dog and keep you company out there at your isolated corner of the world. She's great with other animals, so you could bring her in to work with you."

"You've thought it all through, huh?" Laughing lightly, Ember grasped the dog's face in her hands so they were nose-to-nose. Rather than pull away, "Cujo" relaxed under the pressure of her hands and returned her gaze. "Well, first thing we have to do is give you a proper name."

"Yay!" Bret whooped, high-fiving his brother.

"A name fit for the noble woman that you are," Ember said softly to her new friend. Releasing her, she leaned back and tapped at her chin in thought. After a moment, she snapped her fingers. "Daenerys!"

"Really, Ember?" Becky snorted.

"Don't judge me. So, I enjoy a story about ancient families and epic battles. It's a queen's name, and I like it."

"I think it's cool," Elizabeth offered.

"I don't even allow you to watch the Game of Thrones," Becky reminded her daughter. "But whatever you want, Ember. I'll call her Danny for short."

Smiling at her aunt, Ember was warming up to the idea of having a companion. It had been a long time since she'd been able to keep a pet. Maybe they'd have fun hiking together.

The tune "Staying Alive" suddenly echoed through the room, and Becky began digging in her purse for her phone. Pulling it out, she squinted at the caller ID before accepting the call.

"Hello, this is Becky Stratton of Stratton Animal Rescue Services." Jumping at the screaming on the other end, she held the phone away from her face. "Bonnie? Bonnie, what on earth is the matter? Calm down; I can't understand you!"

Ember could only make out part of the muffled response. Something having to do with a horse and some sort of problem with it.

"Well, that doesn't make any sense. Did something happen?"

As another long string of indistinguishable words came through the line, Becky's brows drew together, and she began chewing at her bottom lip. "Uh-huh. Well, I can't say that I've ever heard of anything like that. I'm not sure what to tell you. Wait!" Turning to Ember, Becky lowered the phone and held it against her chest to mute her end. "I think I have your first client."

TWO

After a rapid exchange on her phone, Becky dropped it into her purse and pulled out her wallet. "Elizabeth, take the boys next door and get some ice cream."

"But, Mom," Elizabeth whined. "You're supposed to drop me off at Heidi's! We *have* to finish planning the parade float this weekend."

"Lizzy, it's Friday." Becky shoved a twenty into her daughter's hand and then made a shooing motion. "You have a week from tomorrow to get that thing done."

When she saw the sincere dejection on Lizzy's face, her features softened. "Look. It's barely nine. I promise we won't be long and I'll have you there before lunch, okay? Something is wrong with the rescue horse you helped me transport to Bonnie's. It's important."

Looking at the money, Elizabeth did some calculations in her head. "Can I have an iced latte?"

Ember stifled a laugh at the wagering. The young teen was just like her mom. Becky always was a shrewd bargainer. When Elizabeth was little, she babysat her all the time. She was only four when Ember moved away. Ever since, she'd only seen the kids on random holidays. Watching the interaction intensified the sense that she'd been missing something important for the past decade. It was good to be home.

"Sure, Lizzy," Becky agreed with an exaggerated tone. "Why don't you get your brothers one other item too. But try not to max out your sugar quota for the month, and *don't* tell your father!"

Leaving them to hammer out the details, Ember jogged to the back office to retrieve her field bag. Walking around the partially-put-together desk she'd just taken out of the box last night, she paused when her hand wrapped around the familiar leather handle. *Dr. Burns, DVM* was burned into the supple leather on the front of the bag, and Ember traced the etching with her free hand. It was a graduation gift from her mom. She'd been so proud.

"Now everyone will know you're a doctor!" her mom had announced, clapping her hands. They'd been sitting in the middle of a restaurant not far from the college campus.

She had hushed her mom. She remembered that now. Why did she do that? Ember's frown turned to a small smile when she recalled the rest of that weekend. Her mom rented a fancy hotel room, and they'd spent two days being pampered with room service and their in-house spa.

A cold nose nudged her wrist, and Ember was pulled from her thoughts. Daenerys was sitting at her feet again, tucked into the small remaining space behind the furniture. Whining softly, the dog looked up at her with a somber expression.

"It's okay," Ember encouraged. "I'm just getting my stuff." Hefting the heavy bag, she grinned and patted at her leg for the Labradoodle to follow.

As they left the room, it dawned on her that Daenerys was already adding a new dimension to her life. She now had someone else to be strong for.

***

"She said the horse was going *crazy*?" Ember navigated around a sharp turn on the two-lane country road. She was familiar with where the farm was but had never met the owner, Bonnie Hathaway. According to Becky, she and her husband had owned for the property for the past five years. Rolling her window down, Ember breathed in the warm summer air. It was heavy with the smell of fresh-cut hay and triggered poignant memories of her time growing up in Sanctuary.

"Yeah. Like I said, it's a rescue horse. But there wasn't anything wrong with it! The vet from Refuge gave him a clean bill of health."

Haven county was made up of three rural communities spaced miles apart through a rugged valley. Sanctuary was the smallest and most central, with Refuge to the North and Parker to the South. One hundred years ago, a group of explorers split off and founded both Sanctuary and Refuge. Sometime later, when logging created a population explosion, Parker arose, named for the owner of the logging company. The debate to change the town's name after Mr. Parker closed shop and left was decades old and still a source of contention among the "old timers."

"Maybe it isn't a physical problem," Ember suggested. "Was it abused?"

"Absolutely not." Becky was resolute. "The woman who surrendered this horse was heartbroken about it. She was a responsible owner and willing to admit, for the sake of the horse, that she couldn't properly care for it anymore. It has a little attitude, but I adore him."

"Okay," Ember replied, surprised at her aunt's emotional response. "I had to ask."

"Of course you did. Sorry if I seem defensive. I feel some guilt over not taking the horse myself, but Paul was adamantly against it.

Ember glanced sideways at her aunt. "Are you guys doing okay?"

"Oh, you don't need to worry about us. Paul's just concerned that I spread myself too thin. As much as I hate to admit he's right … he's right." Chuckling, Becky reached out and patted Ember's leg. "I see that look. Honest, Paul's construction business is booming. The housing market is inflating incredibly fast, although Paul is having to travel farther and farther to find it. But I'm still glad that our valley here is physically inhibited to development to a certain degree. The tourist industry has been more than a substantial source of revenue for the city."

Relieved, Ember was happy to drop the subject and turned her focus back to the horse. Her stomach tightened at the thought of being faced with her first real client. While she had her endorsement to work on horses, it was still new for her. Especially with something this vague. Psychological issues in horses were not easily approached, and it was more likely to be an illness since it came on so suddenly. "How many other horses does Bonnie have?"

"Not many," Becky answered. "They focus on raising Angus cattle and growing alfalfa. I believe they have two or three other horses."

"Do you think she had him in with them yet?"

"No. She was very clear about keeping him quarantined for a week. It's only been a few days."

"That's good." Ember breathed a sigh of relief.

"You're thinking something viral?" Becky questioned, obviously concerned.

"It's impossible to say without examining him. Is this the entrance?" Ember slowed down as they approached a side road with a big log arched entry. "Hathaway Farms" was carved across the top.

Nodding, Becky turned to look at Daenerys in the backseat. "Did I forget to mention Danny's issue with horses?"

"Issue?" Ember said slowly. "What sort of *issue*?"

"The kind you want to avoid. Just don't let her out of the truck. We'll find some shade to park in and leave the windows down. It'll be fine."

Shaking her head, Ember snorted. "Anything else you forgot to mention that I should know about?"

"Nope. She's amazing with people and every animal *except* horses," Becky promised.

Before Ember could push for more of an explanation, a middle-aged woman came running up to greet them as they pulled into a graveled driveway. She looked completely distraught, and the light nerves lingering in Ember's stomach blossomed. Her heartrate doubled, and a cold sweat broke out on her forehead. Distracting herself by gathering her things, she barely remembered to tell Daenerys to stay. Fortunately, the dog *was* well-behaved and remained in the truck as told.

***

The dark-brown quarter horse whipped its head back as they approached the stall, its eyes rolling so that only the whites showed. It screamed in what most closely resembled terror, a sound Ember had never heard before.

"What in the world?" Becky murmured, taking a step back.

"He's frothing, but I can't tell if it's because he's making such a fuss or if he's sick." Bonnie hadn't even waited for introductions but took off for the nearby barn, waving at the two ladies to follow.

Ember took one more cautionary step closer. It was hard to see. The stall was a large 12x24 pen at the back of a typical barn. While there were scattered windows down either side of the open space, the overhead lights were off.

"I thought maybe the dark would help settle him," Bonnie explained when she saw Ember struggling to get a good look. "We've only got but a few horses, so I've kept him quarantined this past week in our foaling stall since it's bigger."

Ember eased past the fretting gelding and walked the length of the pen. She didn't see any other opening. Most stalls had half walls so you could see inside and a secondary entrance if large enough, but this wasn't a typical setup. She could see where the horse might prefer it, but it wasn't very practical from a handling aspect. It would make it extremely difficult to get a lead rope around its neck if their only possible approach was head-on.

"I know," Bonnie said before Ember could comment. "We've talked about modifying this ever since we moved in, but we never had a compelling reason. It wasn't even used prior to Butterscotch."

"You decided to keep his old name?" Becky questioned, smiling at the news in spite of the situation.

"The horse is five. Changing its name would make things even more confusing for him. Not that it likely matters now," Bonnie added while nervously rubbing her hands together, "because he's either gone crazy from the move, or he's very sick."

As if in response, Butterscotch landed a solid kick into the side of the stall, shaking the wall.

Ember went back to stand with the other women. Bonnie was close to tears, but not knowing her, she wasn't sure how to respond. Fortunately, Becky leaned in and wrapped an encouraging arm around her shoulder.

"Where's Carl at, Bonnie?"

"Tending to the cattle. He'll be out most of the day. I tried to call him first, but there are dead spots all over the back forty. I've told that man we need to get some good ole hand-held radios. I've seen some with a three-mile radius that would be more reliable than our darn cell phones!"

"Carl is Bonnie's husband," Becky explained to Ember. "How about that guy you've had helping you out?"

"Unreliable. Tom was supposed to be here at six this morning!" Bonnie pulled away from the embrace and went to retrieve a blinder hanging on the wall with other tack. "I thought that maybe, between the three of us, we could get this on him and it might help calm him."

Blinders were a piece of equipment used to limit a horse's peripheral vision to keep it from getting spooked. But Ember didn't think that was going to be enough. Instead of agreeing, she pointed to a blanket. "Actually, Bonnie, I think the best course of action would be to cover him up completely. That's what we normally do during an exam with a skittish horse. I'm afraid the blinders might make him worse."

Bonnie glanced back and forth between Ember and Becky for a moment. "What do you think, Becky?"

Ember tried not to take the lack of faith in her professional judgment personally. She was new in town, as far as in the capacity of a veterinarian. She was going to have to get used to the skepticism until she'd had a chance to prove herself.

"Of course, there is always a concern that a horse who hasn't been trained to being blinded might react badly," Becky conceded. "But I know the previous owner, and she was responsible. I think Dr. Burns is right. It may be our best bet to get him under control before he hurts himself."

Ember silently thanked her aunt for using her formal title. And she was right. Any good horse owner with a barn should train them in the technique. It was the best way to lead a horse out of a burning barn or away from any sort of threat or danger. But the flip side was that if the horse *wasn't* used to it, the result could be disastrous.

"It looks like he's still reacting to your voice," Ember said encouragingly. "So why don't you try and coax his head out, Bonnie, while Becky and I approach from the sides and place the blanket. Then after you get a rope on him, we'll bring him out where I can give him some medication to calm him and then draw some blood.

Nodding in consent, Bonnie retrieved the lead rope and blanket. There were a few very tense minutes as the three inched their way toward the gelding, Bonnie talking to him quietly the whole time.

"That's a good boy," Bonnie whispered. "We aren't going to hurt you, boy. You know you can trust me."

Butterscotch flared his nostrils and bobbed his head in rapid succession. He stamped at the ground and snorted but didn't back away from the opening. Slowly, carefully, Becky and Ember moved into place. Ember raised her arms as high as she could, holding the bunched-up blanket.

"Now!" Ember silently mouthed around a syringe she had clamped between her teeth. It contained a mild tranquillizer. Reaching out carefully, she gave the free end of the blanket to Becky, who helped direct it down over the horse's head.

At the same time, Bonnie moved in with the rope. Fortunately, Butterscotch responded to the blindness by freezing, allowing Bonnie to secure him. Though he tossed his head at the pressure around his neck, his body visibly relaxed, like he was relieved to relinquish his control to them.

"There you go," Bonnie cooed, still staying as far away as possible while Ember unlatched the gate. "Come on, buddy," she directed, giving the lead a test pull. "Come out here where we can try to help you."

Once Butterscotch started moving, he suddenly ceased struggling after he was out in the openness of the barn. Ember looked questioningly at Becky as she quickly injected the medication, but before she could make a comment, a cell phone rang.

From inside the stall.

It was a distinct tune, but Ember couldn't remember the name of the song, just that it was an 80s classic.

Bonnie's head snapped up. "That's Tom's phone! The man who helps us out around the farm." Pulling urgently on the rope, she led the now-sedated horse to a nearby hitching post.

Stepping into the gloom of the large stall, Ember pulled out her own cell phone and switched on the flashlight app. Becky followed close behind.

"I don't like this," the older woman cautioned. "Something's not right."

Ember nodded slowly in agreement. Stopping about ten feet from the back, she gasped when the light fell upon a boot sticking out of the hay.

"Oh …" Becky moaned, almost falling down when she tried to rapidly scoot backwards. "Call 911, Bonnie!" she yelled.

Grimacing, Ember knelt down near Tom's head. Reaching out, she placed a hand to the side of his throat, confirming what was already obvious. Rocking back on her heels, she looked up at her aunt. "He isn't going to need an ambulance."

THREE

"Well, this is a fine mess." Sheriff Ben Walker grunted as he pushed up from where he'd been squatting next to the body.

"You reckon it was the horse?" The deputy was holding a small digital camera and had just completed taking about a dozen photos.

Ember guessed he was around her age, although she couldn't remember him from school. He'd introduced himself as Deputy Trenton, and the name wasn't familiar. He was tall, skinny, and held himself the way someone does that's worked on a farm all their life. He made a ticking sound against his teeth and then shook his head.

"It sure looks like it was the horse that killed 'im."

"That would be the obvious conclusion," Sheriff Walker said with some irritation. "What's your professional opinion, Dr. Burns?"

Ember was standing at a discreet distance from their "crime scene," as Deputy Trenton had called it when they arrived and shooed everyone out. Becky and Bonnie went inside the farmhouse to try and phone Carl again and make some coffee.

She was absently stroking Butterscotch, having already conducted a thorough exam and drawn what blood she needed. The smell of the leather tack on the wall behind her was comforting, but not enough to ease the ball of anxiety growing in her chest. She couldn't find a thing wrong with him, other than some on-going agitation and rapid heart rate and respirations. His temperature was slightly elevated, but that could be attributed to the stress. She wouldn't know more until she got the blood to a lab.

Ember started slightly when she realized the sheriff was addressing her. She felt uncomfortable being asked to make some sort of determination but figured he was simply feeling out her first impression.

Ben Walker she *did* know. He was her aunt's age, and the two of them had briefly dated when Ember was little. She had fond memories of him, since he'd usually go out of his way to pay attention to her when she was around. He'd always been a large, imposing figure but very friendly and outgoing. A star player on the local football team, he went on to do well at college, which is what eventually drove him and her Aunt Becky apart.

His teeth flashed white against his black skin as he smiled at her hesitation. "I'm not asking for a formal report here, Ember. Off the record. Just a confirmation that what you witnessed when you got here matches up with what appears to be this poor man's demise."

"I would say so, Sheriff," she said softly. She wasn't sure why she was nearly whispering. Maybe it was the same sense as being in a church. Having a man's body lying there like that made the room feel … consecrated, so that she needed to be respectful. It was an odd experience, and one she hoped to never go through again.

Sensing her unease, Sheriff Walker exited the stall and approached where the horse was still tethered, halfway down the length of the barn. The deputy followed and began taking pictures of Butterscotch.

Hooking his thumbs through a black leather gun belt that rested over his blue jeans, Walker looked down at his cowboy boots and frowned. "His name is Tom Clark. His wife called this morning to report him missing. Dammit!" Removing the department-issued hat from his head, he wiped at his brow. "That isn't a house call I'm looking forward to making. They've got two kids. Ken," he barked, revealing his deputies first name, "better give Doc Austin a call."

"Why call a doctor out here?" Ember questioned. She understood why the dispatcher originally sent an ambulance, but the paramedic already officially called the death, based on the obvious head trauma.

"Doctor Sean Austin runs the medical clinic in town, and he's also the elected Coroner for the county," Walker explained.

"I believe the medics already requested dispatch to get him for us," the deputy replied. "But I'll make sure." Unclipping a radio from his hip, Ken made his way toward the exit.

While the sheriff apparently had some leeway on what he chose to wear, the deputy was in full formal attire. Walker had also arrived in a plain-marked SUV with only "Haven County Sheriff" emblazoned on the door, while Ken was driving a regular police car. As she watched him walk outside, another one pulled up and he waved at whoever was driving.

"How many officers are working for you?" Ember asked. The county itself was very spread out, and she imagined it would be a challenge to patrol it. The main police station was located in Sanctuary, likely because of its central location, but she thought there were also a couple of satellite offices in the other towns.

"I have two deputies here and eight more assigned to the other regions. We've finally gotten to where we have at least four officers covering Haven County at all times. It was a challenge convincing some of the councilmembers of the need, but the population has been steadily growing, especially in Parker. I imagine they may end up forming a city agency there before too long." Pausing, Sheriff Walker gestured to the blood tubes Ember was still holding. "You think that's going to tell us why the horse went homicidal?"

Ember cringed at the term, concerned at what might happen to the animal. "I hope so," she said with some trepidation.

"So now what? If it isn't an illness that can be treated that drove him to kick a man to death, what do you do with him? Put him down?"

Great, Ember thought. *My first day on the job and I'm already in a situation I have no clue how to handle.* She decided to be honest.

"I don't know. I'm going to have to make some phone calls to get some advice. My exam is inconclusive, and while he's much calmer, that may just be from the tranquillizer. For now, I'll suggest he be kept in quarantine with continued sedation until the lab work comes back."

"Can horses get rabies?"

Ember looked at Sheriff Walker, not wanting to reveal that he'd voiced her primary concern. Rabies was rare but not unheard of, even in vaccinated horses.

"Of course they can get rabies, Ben," an unknown voice interrupted. "I know you weren't raised on a farm, but I figured even *you* would know that."

Ember squinted as the bright light coming in through the open barn doors turned the approaching man into a silhouette. He was tall with broad shoulders, and as he walked under the first light, Ember surmised that he must be Dr. Austin. He had classic good looks with blonde hair, an aristocratic nose, and blue eyes that shone with intelligence. He wore a white lab coat with the name "Haven Medical Clinic" stitched over the breast pocket.

"As pompous as ever," Walker mumbled, but it was obvious the two men were friends by the way they shook hands.

"He's right," Ember confirmed. "It's one of the viruses I'm testing for. I'm Dr. Burns," she continued, turning her attention to the new arrival. As the full weight of his gaze fell on her, she could feel a wall start to go up, and she fought against it. Something about good-looking men made her defensive. Especially smart ones. It was a character flaw she'd struggled with since high school. She didn't even have a nasty breakup story to justify it.

"That's right; you're the new vet in town!" Reaching out, he gave her a solid handshake. "I didn't think you were opening your doors for another week or two. I'm Dr. Austin, but please, call me Sean."

Blushing slightly in spite of her attempt to remain emotionally neutral, Ember had to admit that he seemed like a down-to-earth guy. "Technically, I'm *not* open yet. I have my business license, and everything else in place; but the clinic is still a mess. My aunt runs the local animal shelter and got the original call about the horse. She asked for my help, so I came out." Desperate for an excuse to look away from his direct stare, she resumed rubbing

Butterscotch's neck and then began re-examining him, starting with his eyes.

Moving up behind her, Sean leaned forward to get his own look at the horse. "Did you sedate him?"

"Yes. Just enough to keep him from hurting himself or anyone else."

Nodding in approval, Sean stepped back and crossed his arms over his chest. "I've been the county coroner for two years now, and I have to say that this will likely go down as the strangest case."

"I hear ya, Doc," Walker chimed in. "Deputy Trenton will help you remove the body—"

"Sheriff Walker! What is going on?"

Ember grabbed the lead rope as Butterscotch reared back, shying away from the loud voice. Stomping into the barn was a large middle-aged man. His work clothes were covered in dirt, and Ember figured he had to be Carl Hathaway.

"Carl, I told you on the phone not to go making a big fuss out here!" Bonnie ran in after her husband, a steaming mug of coffee in each hand. "Now you've spooked the horse!"

"Spooked the horse?" Carl yelled in disbelief. "There's a man lying dead in our barn, and your concern right now is that I *don't spook the horse*?" Pulling off his leather work gloves, Carl glared at the horse in question before accepting the coffee his wife held out patiently. It appeared that the two were used to tumultuous exchanges. "I told you we didn't need another horse!"

"Carl Hathaway, I was here the day you took that horse in, and *you* were the one to make the final decision to keep him." Becky had followed the couple inside, and Ember recognized the look of determination on her aunt's face.

Uh-oh. Time for an intervention. "Aunt Becky, can you please bring me some of that coffee?" Ember knew she was being obvious but didn't care. Emotions were running high, and it wasn't the right time for the conversation of who was at fault.

Becky hesitated, but then her expression changed as she came to the same conclusion. "I'm sorry, Carl," she said as she walked past him. "I know Tom was a friend. This is a crummy situation all-around."

Carl's shoulders sagged, and he nodded silently. Avoiding looking at the stall, he turned to the sheriff. "Just tell me what happened, Walker."

"I wish I could, Carl." Gesturing for his deputy to take the doctor back to where Tom was, he then focused on the older man. "It looks like Tom was in working on the gelding's shoes. His tools were set out. We don't know why, but for whatever reason, the horse managed to trample him."

"Tom is … *was* an experienced and certified farrier," Carl stated. "He was planning on shoeing him this week, but when I closed up the barn last night at six, he wasn't here."

Sheriff Walker removed a small pad of paper from his back pocket and took some notes. "So, you say he wasn't here at six? Did anyone see him after that time?"

Ember watched the exchange silently. A farrier was someone who specialized in hoof care. It wasn't regulated in the United States, but there were some associations that would give accreditation with specific requirements. Carl was right; someone who went to the length of certification was good at what they did. Looking at Butterscotch, Ember had a growing sense of unease.

"He's been doing extra work around the place for us a couple days a week," Bonnie offered. "But he's normally gone by five. I didn't see him leave last night, but that wasn't unusual. Sometimes he'd be on the back forty and then just go home from there. Ya know his place is only a few miles away. His wife, Vanessa, dropped him off yesterday, and he was going to walk home. Oh, no!" Bonnie gasped, covering her mouth with her hand. "That poor girl. Does she know? Has anyone told her yet?"

"I'm going to go notify her when we're done talking," the sheriff said, scribbling down something else. "I want to make sure I understand as much as I can before I speak with her. Have you had any further trouble with Tom like you did last year?"

Bonnie looked uncomfortable with the question, and Carl's face reddened. "I don't see why you need to ask something like that," he growled.

"Because it's my job. Now, I know you chose not to press charges, but the equipment you caught him stealing was worth a lot of money. I respect the fact that you wanted to help him and his family get through a rough spot, but I have to ask. Have you had any other altercations with him, Carl?"

Ember did her best to busy herself with putting things away in her bag so it wouldn't appear that she was paying attention, but Becky didn't have the same concern. Tsking in disapproval, she placed her hands on her hips and interjected. "I heard that he'd gotten sucked into that casino in Parker. Spent all the mortgage money a month before Christmas last year. It was kind of you to help him, Bonnie. I know Tom spoke to my husband just a few weeks ago about putting up a garage, so I figured they were doing well now."

"They were," Bonnie agreed. Placing a calming hand on her husband's arm, she answered the question for him. "We never regretted our decision, Sheriff. Tom was a good worker, and he never gave us any more trouble. He's been getting lots of work lately at another ranch."

"Maybe he came back later in the evening to get a jump on his workload," the sheriff suggested.

"He was tired," Ember added, "and got caught off guard by a sick horse."

"Sounds plausible," Carl agreed, visibly relaxing.

"I'd say it sounds *very* plausible," Dr. Austin offered, joining the group. His hands were gloved, and his expression was grim. "I'll have to do a more thorough exam before writing up an official report, but I think it's obvious the cause of death is blunt-force trauma to the head."

"What are you going to do about the horse?" Carl demanded, turning on Ember.

Ember straightened and tried not to look as dismayed as she felt. There was a very good chance she wasn't going to be able to save the life of her first client.

FOUR

Becky had her door open before the truck even finished pulling up to the clinic. "If I *really* hurry, I might still pull off a miracle and get Lizzy to her friend's by noon," she called back to Ember as her feet hit the pavement.

Ember was too emotionally drained to laugh, but she still smiled at her aunt's antics. She couldn't fathom how much Becky still had to do that afternoon, and it didn't appear she was thrown off at all by the scene they just left. Ember knew that wasn't true. It was a unique ability most mothers had to keep going in spite of how or what they felt. *She* planned on making a very strong pot of coffee and eating something sweet and fattening.

"Here! I almost forgot to give this to you."

Ember jumped at the abrupt reappearance of Becky at the passenger door. She was holding a large cloth grocery bag overflowing with what looked like stuffed animals.

"What's that?" she asked, turning the truck off and pulling the keys out of the ignition.

"Danny's stuff. Harness, leash, bowls, small bag of food, brush, and toys. I forgot the bed."

Ember realized that Becky was serious. "Beck, I *sell* dog beds. We'll manage. And do me a favor and take a deep breath or something."

Shaking her head, Becky dropped the bag on the seat. "I'm fine. But I have a date with a bottle of red wine and a hot bath later tonight. A *large* bottle." She started to turn away again but then paused and looked back for a second time. "I want to apologize for dragging you into this. I shouldn't have asked you to go out there when you aren't even open for business."

Jumping out of the truck, Ember walked around to the other side and gave her aunt a big hug. "I'm glad I was able to help. You couldn't have known what was going to happen, so don't give that another thought, okay?"

Nodding, Becky returned the embrace. "All right. Gotta run. Give me a call if anything else happens or you have a question about Dann—umm … Daenerys."

Grinning, Ember dug in the bag for a squeaky toy. "Don't worry about us." Pulling out a rubber bone, she motioned for Daenerys to come. The dog happily leapt down from the truck and snatched the toy from her hand. "I'll check in with you later tonight."

Waving goodbye, Becky hopped in her SUV and sped across the street to the coffee shop where her children were waiting, likely in need of a sugar detox.

Still trying to steady her nerves, Ember reached back into the truck for the leather physician's satchel and the blood samples it contained. A lot was riding on the test results, so she wanted to get them to the lab in Parker ASAP. She and Becky stayed with Bonnie for a full hour after the coroner and police left. Ember tended to Butterscotch and made sure he was settled into a new stall while Becky made lunch for the owners. For whatever reason, the impact of horrific events can usually be lightened by holding a warm drink and eating some comforting food.

Embers stomach rumbled, reminding her that she hadn't eaten yet. After caring for the gelding, she waited for Becky in the truck with Daenerys. She'd already felt bad about leaving her in the vehicle for as long as she had and wasn't going to totally abandon her. Fortunately, the morning didn't start off as hot as the day before, and there were plenty of trees to park under. One of the first things she needed to do was to make a space for Daenerys in her office. She wouldn't be able to take her on any more house calls.

"Ahem."

Jerked from her thoughts, Ember looked up to discover a young woman sitting on the front step of the clinic. She appeared to be in her mid-twenties and was very petite with dark brown hair and matching eyes. The main entrance was slightly recessed, so Ember hadn't spotted her before. She experienced a brief moment of confusion before recognizing the visitor. Dr. Bernie had two previous employees: an elderly receptionist who retired at the same time and wasn't interested in coming to work for her, and an eager local girl who recently completed her Veterinary Technician certification. Ember emailed her last week and had gotten a response right away, which included her profile picture. They'd set up a time to meet and discuss the possibility of her coming to work at the clinic.

"Oh my gosh!" Ember gasped. Rushing forward, she set her bag on the sidewalk and reached out a hand. "Are you Michelle Johns? This morning did *not* go as planned, and I'm embarrassed to admit that I totally forgot about our meeting."

Michelle surprised Ember by grasping onto her offered hand and using it to pull herself up instead of shaking it. "No worries. I found Elizabeth and the boys next door, and she told me you and Becky took off for the Hathaways' place. Is everything okay? I saw a couple of cops heading out that direction on my way over here. And please, everyone calls me Mel. It's easier to say."

Ember always relied heavily on her first impression of a person and found her initial instinct was usually correct. She liked Mel. Her voice was deeper than expected, and she was even smaller standing than she appeared when sitting. However, she was one of those people whose personality filled a room, and Ember had always been attracted to that type. They were fun to be around.

Encouraged by the prospect of having a good employee and co-worker, Ember returned the smile. Becky was the one who gave her Mel's email address and recommendation. The animal shelter and veterinarian always worked closely together.

A young couple walked past them, obvious tourists with shopping bags and the "on vacation" glow about them. The woman nodded a greeting to them before stopping to pet the tail-wagging labradoodle.

Suddenly aware of several other people strolling about and cars driving by, Ember felt a need to be discreet about what happened at the farm. Grabbing her bag, she unlocked the front door. "Let's talk about it inside," she told a patiently waiting Mel.

One of the features Ember liked best about the clinic was the fact that it was a single-story, stand-alone unit. All of the buildings on the block were considered one of the "newer" sections of town, having been built in the early 1970s. Dr. Bernie liked to brag about how he purchased it brand-new. It was an attractive small brick structure without either a basement or upstairs and had a nice patch of grass in the back along the alley. While the façade still matched the original buildings on the next block over, those all had at least two stories and often featured the store on the main floor and apartments above or below.

Ember's clinic was on the corner, so the charming coffee shop and bakery was to the right of it, across the street. On the left side of the clinic was a popular gift shop filled with all of the expected keepsakes vacationers longed for. In addition to the souvenirs, the owners also set up a photoshoot area in the back, complete with authentic western-style costumes. It was a popular destination, so there was plenty of foot traffic on the sidewalk.

Not needing any further explanation, Mel followed Ember inside and immediately went for the dog treats. "What did you name her?" she asked, kneeling down with the milk bone. "And please don't tell me you're going with Cujo, because I told Becky that no respectable person would do that to this beautiful girl."

"I agree," Ember laughed. She headed for the back counter and went about making the pot of coffee she was daydreaming of. "I decided on Daenerys—wait! You said you saw the police responding on your way *over* here. Have you really been sitting on that step for two hours?"

"Gosh, no!" Mel retorted. "I have to confess that I live in a small apartment under the coffee shop. I sat with the kids and helped dose them up with caffeine and then came over after Becky messaged Elizabeth that you were on your way back. But if the sympathy vote helps me get a job, then sure; I was sitting on the step for two hours."

"The snark is strong in you, young Padawan," Ember teased, warming up to Mel immediately.

"Whoa, Game of Thrones *and* Star Wars references?" Mel gasped. "You and I are going to get along famously!"

The fact that Mel *got* both of her geeky insinuations was all the confirmation that Ember needed. She already knew that she'd be a good employee based on Becky's referral. "I know what Bernie was paying you," Ember said, getting right to the point. "I'll give you two dollars more an hour. Plus, I need you to work full-time at forty hours a week instead of the thirty you were doing for him. I can't offer you insurance, but you'll accrue one day of sick leave and one day of vacation a month, starting immediately. I'm pretty laid back, and all I ask is for good work ethic and professionalism. Well, at least while we're in front of customers," she added, conscious of the joking she'd just done.

"Just like that?" Mel asked, standing to face Ember. "You don't want to sit me down and grill me about my parents or schooling or sordid breakup with the sheriff's son?"

Crossing her arms, Ember leaned back against the counter while the thick aroma of coffee began to fill the room. "Is there anything I need to know?"

"Well," Mel began, hopping onto the counter and sitting cross-legged across from Ember. "I grew up in Refuge, and my parents are still there. My dad's a pastor, and my mom's a school bus driver. Don't laugh. I started working for Doc Bernie when I was twenty-two. He was very supportive in helping me get my certification, although it took me three years to complete a two-year program. I never actually dated the sheriff's son. But even though he breaks my 'no dating men more than two years younger' rule at twenty-two, I would totally say yes if he ever asked me out."

"Anything else?" Ember questioned, openly laughing.

"I'm a hard worker. I love animals, and I'm fiercely loyal. I may look small, but I can lift a dog half my size."

"Wonderful. You're hired!" Stepping forward at the same time Mel jumped off the counter, the two women exchanged a firm handshake.

"Thanks, Dr. Burns!" Mel nearly bounced with joy. "I practiced my speech in front of a mirror for a whole week, so I appreciate you letting me deliver it. Otherwise, I would have been beating myself up over the unnecessary stress I caused myself."

"Honestly, Mel, I don't know if you're going to be as happy after this next week. There's a ton of work to do, and other than Becky helping out when she can, we're going to be on our own. I wish I could afford to pay you more, because I feel like I'm going to be asking you to step into a pretty big role as not only my technician but the office manager too."

"I do better under stress," Mel replied without any hesitation. "Marissa ran the office for, like, thirty years. But I was the only one here on weekends, so I know how to do it. My only confession is that I'm a complete coffee addict. Renting the apartment next door was a near-fatal move in that I now operate on a completely different level. Seriously. I've already downed two iced lattes today, but I'm all about having a huge cup of that pot you just brewed. What brand is that? It smells incredible!"

For some reason, Ember was glad to learn Mel also enjoyed coffee. Sanctuary wasn't quite up to speed with the coffee craze taking over the western half of Washington State, and there were only a couple of shops.

"I found this blend a few months ago at a small store when I was hiking some trails at Mount Rainier. I've been saving it, since I knew the selection wasn't that vast out here yet."

"One day, I'm going to open my own stand here," Mel stated. After accepting the offered cup from Ember, she doctored it up with some French vanilla creamer. "Can you imagine how popular it would be in the summer with the tourists? Especially on the outskirts of town where you can easily pull in and out." Sniffing the brew first, she then took a slow sip. "Mmm, you're right. This is heavenly. So," she added, "when do I start? And are you going to tell me what happened out at Bonnie's?"

"The clinic doesn't officially open until a week from this coming Monday, but if you can start now, I have some samples for you to take to the lab in Parker for me," Ember replied, digging in her bag for the vials. "As for Bonnie's …" Hesitating, she debated how to say it. "There was an accident. A really *bad* accident. We need to keep this under wraps for now because it's still being investigated, okay?"

"Okay …" Mel said slowly, encouraging Ember to continue.

"There's no easy way to say it. Butterscotch was freaking out, and when we got him out of his stall, Becky and I found Tom Clark's body. It looked like he was trampled to death."

Pausing with the mug up to her mouth, Mel's eyes got wide. She slowly lowered it without taking another drink. "Well. I would have *never* guessed that!"

"Do you know Tom?"

"I know who he is," Mel answered. "But I don't—didn't—know him. I moved to Sanctuary just this past year, after I finished school, because the commute was closer from Refuge. I'm still considered an 'outsider.'"

Ember knew exactly what Mel was talking about. In such a small community, acceptance was slow in being earned. Even though Ember was born and raised there, many would view her as a traitor for moving away for so long. It would take time before she was welcomed back into some of those tight circles.

"Are you sure he was *trampled*? I mean, the guy was a farrier, so he obviously knew how to handle a horse. That doesn't make any sense. Didn't Bonnie know he was there?"

"Trust me," Ember breathed, tossing another toy out for Daenerys. "There are a ton more questions than there are answers. Butterscotch calmed down a lot once we got him out and sedated him, but his vitals were off. Not a lot, but enough to make me suspicious. That's why it's so important to get the blood to the lab right away. I know we won't get results until after the weekend, but I want to at least get it there."

"Are you thinking rabies?" Mel glanced at Ember's hands and then moved her coffee cup farther from her face.

"Yeah, but don't worry. I gloved up and also washed my hands several times before I left. Plus, he didn't have a high fever or exhibit several of the classic signs of rabies."

"Maybe meningitis or a brain tumor or something else that could affect his brain," Mel mumbled, thinking out loud.

"Yeah, a virus crossing the blood-brain barrier is my top suspect, but I hadn't thought of a tumor. If the blood comes up negative and he's still displaying symptoms, we could suggest a brain scan. Good thinking!"

"Thanks, Dr. Burns," Mel replied, blushing slightly. "I can leave now, if you like. Did you already contract with the lab for services? Because they have order slips that need to be filled out."

"Oh, yeah! I have a pad of them in my office. I'll go get one. And, Mel, you can call me Ember when we don't have anyone here. I still feel funny being called doctor at all, but I know it lends a certain amount of credibility when the clients hear the title."

"A well-earned title," Mel countered. "I could never go to school for that long, or handle the classes. People don't realize it requires the same level of training as a human doctor!"

"Thanks," Ember said with genuine gratitude. It was nice to have someone around who understood what was involved in her career. "When you get back, maybe you can help me figure out how to finish putting my stupid desk together, and then I'll buy you a 'welcome aboard' dinner."

Before Mel had a chance to answer, there was a pounding at the front door. Both ladies jumped, but Ember recovered first. Glad that she thought to lock the door behind them, she went and peeked out through the pulled blinds on the large window beside the door.

Sheriff Walker stared back.

Fumbling with the deadbolt, she was thoroughly embarrassed by the time she got the door open.

"You know we have a nearly non-existent crime level here, right?" he asked, a grin on his broad face.

"Habit. What's up?"

"Dr. Austin sent me over," Walker explained. "Neither one of us has your cell number, and you didn't give me your statement yet."

"Oh." Ember had promised to turn in the witness account by the next day. "If you have a few minutes, I can finish writing it up now."

"No, that's not why I'm here." Glancing at Mel, he gave her a nod. "Hello, Mel."

"Hey, Sheriff! How's Cody?"

Shaking his head, Walker ignored the question about his son and turned back to Ember. "I need you to come back with me to the clinic."

"Why?" Ember asked, confused.

"Because Sean is finishing up with his exam, and he needs you to observe as a professional witness."

FIVE

Ember leaned against the wall in the farthest corner of the room she could find. Even though Sean was only conducting an exam and not an autopsy—since he wasn't a certified medical examiner or forensics pathologist—it wasn't where Ember wanted to be. She'd had to sit in on such things as a student and found it nightmare-inducing. The sooner they got to the point of why she was there, the better.

Seeing Dr. Sean Austin in his element was somewhat intimidating. The clinic was a far cry from a large hospital, but it was still impressive, especially for Sanctuary. An ornate plaque prominently placed near the entrance had a short list of benefactors.

"How many employees do you have here?" Ember asked, desperate to fill the silence and take her mind off the body on the table. Sean and Sheriff Walker were huddled on the other side of the exam room, apparently going over the report.

Glancing up at her, Sean flashed a warm smile. "I have three other doctors, a physician's assistant, and two nurses working for me. We've got a portable x-ray machine and even a refurbished CAT scan. Only thing we have to send our patients away for is an MRI. While we can deal with most minor emergencies, anything surgical or needing admission is transferred to the nearest receiving facility. Between the two other private practices here in Sanctuary, we keep our community pretty well covered."

Ember wasn't sure why, but his reply felt canned, like he'd rehearsed it for a commercial. But he was so charming that she found herself smiling back like he'd just revealed some great secret.

Irritated at the way her pulse sped up in response to his attention, she pointed at the papers in his hand instead of embarrassing herself by gushing compliments. "Is that what you want me to sign? Because I already started writing up my statement from this morning." She was eager to get back to her clinic. She'd closed Daenerys in her office with a large dog bed and a bowl of water, but there was no guarantee she wasn't already chewing on a leg of her new desk.

"Yes," he answered, not missing a beat. "However, it's different from the witness form. This is my medical examination report. As you know, since I'm not a pathologist, I can only sign death certificates for natural or accidental causes. Anything requiring further scrutiny has to be sent out, and this case is borderline. Tom's wife, Vanessa, is vehemently against an autopsy being conducted. A lot of people feel the same way, and I understand how painful this all is for her. To avoid any push-back from the state, I figured it would help to have a professional witness attest to the fact that a horse did, in fact, cause the death."

Crossing the short distance between them, Sean handed her the three-page document and a pen. Skipping to the last page, Ember turned to use the wall to sign against. As she stood with the pen hovering over the line, she read through the statement she was attesting to, which was conveniently filled in for her:

I, Ember Burns, bear witness to the examination of Thomas Clark and confirm to the best of my knowledge as a DVM, certified in the State of Washington, that the most likely cause of death was blunt-force trauma to the head, which was done by a horse in his stall while Mr. Clark was working in his profession as a farrier.

Ember paused. By signing, she could very well also be signing Butterscotch's death certificate, and she hadn't actually seen any of the exam. The horse was her patient, and he was still alive. She owed it to him to be truthful and thorough. As much as she hated the idea, she lowered the papers and turned back to Sean.

"I'm sure I won't come to any other conclusion, but I think I should examine the … body, before I sign this."

Sean's smile faltered. He didn't take the statement back. "Dr. Burns, if you already know what you're going to find, then why put yourself through it? I can assure you that there's nothing to gain by it."

"Please, you can call me Ember. And I'm sure you're right, but I still have the horse to deal with. If there's *any* chance he didn't do this, I would be negligent to not take the time to make sure."

Nodding in understanding, the doctor seemed to relax a little with the explanation. Ember wondered if his ego was really that big or if it was the opposite and he thought she was questioning his judgment. Either way, she couldn't be concerned about his feelings at the moment.

Moving forward, she donned some nitrile gloves and began to look over the wounds, tentatively at first but then with growing interest. There were several blows to the head that could have been fatal, but there was little bruising other than around one eye and along the jawline. His chest was unremarkable.

Straightening, Ember saw that both Dr. Austin and Sheriff Walker were watching her. Blushing slightly, she decided to go all-in. "Can you help me roll him?"

"*Roll* him?" Sean repeated.

"Yeah. I'd like to see his back."

"Is that really necessary?" Walker asked, looking put out.

Feeling the first stirrings of irritation, Ember began to roll him herself. “Look, you guys are the ones that asked me to sign my name to an official document. So don’t act like I’m the one being unreasonable.”

Shrugging, Sean stepped up to the other side of the table and took over the task, directing the sheriff to help. “She’s right,” he said, surprising her. “Ember, I shouldn’t have asked you to sign that without having you here for the whole procedure. I made the assumption that you would prefer not to take part, but I was clearly mistaken.”

Satisfied with the apology, Ember simply smiled in response and then continued her investigation. Aside from some abrasions, Sean was right, and his back was unremarkable too. Leaning in for a closer look at the cuts to see if there was any sign of bleeding to indicate if they happened prior to or after death, Ember noticed something odd. While most of the scratches were ragged, there was one that stood out. She had always had a knack for patterns, or anything that didn’t *fit* a pattern. One particular mark was small, straight, and very precise. It also had a defined area of bruising and inflammation around it that was different from the rest.

Reaching out, Ember traced a gloved finger along it. It was no more than an inch in length, located just below the shoulder blade and in between two ribs on the left side. Placing her other hand on the opposite side of the wound, she pulled the two edges apart, revealing a deep laceration or puncture. *Very* deep.

"What's that?" Walker demanded, suddenly interested.

"Maybe he fell against something in the stall?" Sean offered, also moving in closer to scrutinize it.

"Well, whatever made that cut was extremely sharp," Walker observed. "And I don't recall seeing anything in the stall that would account for it."

"What about the farrier tools?" Sean pressed. "A couple of those chisels might be about the right size."

"What about his shirt?" Ember suggested. "Lay it out. Let's see what kind of cut there is on it and how much blood."

"Whoa …" Walker called out, holding his hands up to stop Sean from touching the shirt. "Sean, I'm sorry, but you know what this means."

Sean and Ember looked at each other and then back at the sheriff. The slow realization of what her discovery just triggered caused a new knot of anxiety to spring to life in Ember's stomach.

"I'm going to have to confiscate all of his belongings as evidence and turn his body over to the state for an autopsy and complete forensics analysis," Sheriff Walker spelled out for them. "This is now a potential murder investigation."

SIX

The sun was painting a colorful pallet in the sky by the time Ember drove back out to Bonnie and Carl's place. It wasn't exactly on her way home, but she didn't have to go too far out of her way.

Mel had been sitting on the step of the clinic again when she'd returned earlier, and it was decided that the first order of business was to have some keys made. That, and tackling the desk was all they had time for. Mel got called to her parents, so they decided to do dinner another night.

Ember already planned to check in on Butterscotch, but she was debating what exactly to say to Bonnie. Everything was speculation at that point. It could still go either way: a sick horse or a murderer on the loose. If it were the later, she realized, there was no way of knowing *who* the killer was. Except that they went to some extremes to try and cover it up. And it could be anyone.

"Get a grip, Burns," Ember muttered out loud, causing Daenerys to whimper in response and tilt her head sideways. "It's okay, girl," Ember cooed. "I'm just doing a good job of freaking myself out."

Her cell phone took that opportune moment to ring, making her jump, and Daenerys bark. Laughing, Ember concentrated on not weaving in her lane. Fortunately, they were approaching the entrance to the ranch, so she pulled over and stopped under the big archway. The old truck had nothing resembling Bluetooth, so she dug her phone out of her pocket on the fifth ring and held it to her ear.

"Hello? This is Dr. Burns."

"Hey, uh … Ember. This is Sean. I hope you don't mind that I got your number off your statement."

Instantly concerned, Ember's brow furrowed. *Why* would Dr. Austin be calling her? She left his office feeling extremely awkward, unsure of whether she had potentially made a vital discovery or simply caused a hard situation to be even more difficult.

"No, that's fine," she replied with some hesitation. "What can I do for you, Dr. Austin?"

There was a pause.

Good, he noticed I'm keeping things formal.

"Ember, I feel like the circumstances we've met under have gotten us off to a wrong start. I'd like to correct that. Maybe over dinner tomorrow night? And please, call me Sean."

Completely taken off guard, Ember stuttered, "I … um … well, I suppose." Instantly chastising herself, Ember looked accusingly at Daenerys for not stopping her. "What I mean, is—"

"Good!" Sean interrupted, not giving her a chance to recant her acceptance. "Will you be in town tomorrow? If so, I can pick you up at your office around five."

Letting out a sigh of defeat, Ember closed her eyes. "Sure. I'll be there around that time, but I won't be dressed very nice." Maybe she could convince him she would be an embarrassment to take out in public.

Laughing, Sean didn't miss a beat. "I don't think there's anywhere in Sanctuary that has a dress code."

Ember couldn't help but notice what a nice laugh he had. Easy, and rich. Maybe she'd misread him earlier. It *was* under some weird circumstances. He could be right, that they needed to reintroduce themselves in a more … *normal* situation. Brightening a little at the thought, she smiled at Daenerys, who was sitting in the passenger seat next to her, drooling on her purse.

"Thank you for the invitation, *Sean*," she replied, emphasizing his name. "I'll see you tomorrow at five."

After hanging up, she sat staring at the phone for a full minute. She had no plans to start dating him or anyone else in the near future, but dinner might be nice. And he was nice to look at.

Daenerys whined at her again.

"What?" she laughed, rubbing the dog behind the ears. It quickly became apparent throughout the day that this was her favorite spot to have scratched. "So what if I'm sitting along the side of a road in a running truck, staring at my phone? Nothing at all unusual about that." After putting the truck back into drive, she continued down the driveway. "And now I'm talking to my dog," she muttered.

Pulling up under the same shade tree she'd been parked under earlier, Ember ordered Daenerys to stay, feeling guilty. "It's only for a few minutes this time," she promised, while digging out yet another dog treat. She was going to have to buy more.

Bonnie came out to meet her, and Ember was concerned by the expression on the older woman's face. Something else must have happened with Butterscotch. "What's wrong?" Ember asked, turning toward the barn.

"Hold on," Bonnie ordered, sticking out a hand to stop Ember. "There's nothing wrong with the horse."

Stopping at the tone of her voice, Ember once again had a bad feeling. "He's doing better?" she asked, trying not to read too much into the way Bonnie was standing with her hands on her hips. She looked worried.

"Well, of course he's doing better! Now that the drugs you gave him have worn off. I should have known to question it, given the history of your predecessor."

Bristling at the accusatory nature of the comment, Ember went on the defensive. "Look, Bonnie, I don't know what's going on, or what you're referring to, but you and I both know that Butterscotch was having an issue this morning long before I got here. Those *drugs* are what calmed him down!"

"Maybe," Bonnie conceded, "but don't you think that maybe the horse was simply reacting to the man in his stall that was *murdered*?"

"Who told you that?" Ember shot back, knowing that getting into an argument with the woman wasn't going to help anything, but she was unable to stop herself. She had a quick temper with certain triggers, and someone accusing her of wrongly caring for an animal was a big one.

"The sheriff left here about a half-hour ago," Bonnie explained. "I know that this is now a *murder* investigation! Some men from State Patrol came in with a bunch of fancy equipment to lift prints or something, and then they spent nearly an hour questioning us. *Us,* Dr. Burns, like we're some sort of suspects!"

Ember's anger was gone as fast as it sparked. The woman was terrified, that's all. Putting a hand on her shoulder, she did her best to placate her. "Bonnie, it's all circumstantial. They won't know the real cause of death for several days. The wound may have been from anything and incidental to his being … trampled."

"Why are you so eager to accuse that horse?" Bonnie countered, surprising Ember again with her attitude. "You were the one that indicated to the police this morning that he could have done it. Is there really even anything wrong with him? Because he seems to be acting fine to me now."

"Bonnie, I'm not eager to accuse anyone of anything. I just want to make sure we know all the facts before coming to any conclusions. We won't have his bloodwork back until Monday or Tuesday. His vitals *were* off this morning, which is why I would really like to examine him again. If he's doing better, like you say, then that's a great sign. And I'm the one who discovered that wound, so please trust that I'm doing all I can to make sure your horse isn't accused of something it didn't do."

"You mean to say *you're* the one that caused the huge mess here this afternoon?" Bonnie exploded, waving her hands in the air.

Ember was completely exasperated. Nothing she said was going to satisfy this woman. Trying to control her reaction, she reminded herself why she was there. "Like I said, I just want to make sure that the truth is known. I'm sure that's all anyone wants, including you and Tom's wife."

Bonnie relaxed a little, apparently unable to find a reason to argue against that.

"Can I please just check on him?" Ember pressed, seeing an opening. "I won't give him any more sedatives if that's what you want. But I'd like to document his vitals and current behavior. I'm trying to help him," she added, hoping that Bonnie would be reasonable.

Bonnie's shoulders sagged. "I know you are, Dr. Burns," she admitted, shaking her head. "I don't even know what I'm thinking anymore. I'm sorry. I just—go on. Go look at him, will you? Then I don't want to think about any of this for the rest of the night."

Not needing any further prompting, Ember headed for the barn. Stepping inside, she saw there was police tape across the opening to the stall. Butterscotch was now housed in a smaller one, closer to the barn door. He stood quietly, looking at her.

Approaching him cautiously at first, since the sedative should have nearly worked its way completely out of his system by then, Ember could tell right away that Bonnie was right. There was absolutely no sign of any agitation. Going to work, it only took a few minutes to determine that all his vital signs were perfectly normal.

Leaning against the stall door, she studied the horse. He stared back at Ember, his large brown eyes reflecting her image. Blinking slowly, Butterscotch gently stretched his head forward and then rested it on her shoulder. It was the same gesture her horse used to do when she was a child. Touched, Ember reached up and stroked the gelding's neck while speaking softly to him.

"It's okay, boy. Nothing's going to happen to you. I'll make sure of it."

Even without the bloodwork results, it was clear to Ember that the horse wasn't sick. That made the likelihood of him being responsible for Tom's death extremely unlikely. Horses were known to avoid stepping on people lying on the ground. When it did happen, it was usually accidental. It was an instinct thing, to prevent them from breaking a leg. Even in a small space, provoked, Ember couldn't buy into the whole trampling thing *unless* the horse was very ill. That morning, he certainly was behaving like he was crazed. None of it made sense.

Tossing his head, Butterscotch took a step back and snorted, making Ember laugh.

"I guess the conversation is over!" she said, gathering her things. "I'll see you tomorrow."

Back outside, she didn't see Bonnie anywhere, so she headed for her truck. As she was standing with the door open, setting her bag in the small backseat area of the extended cab, Carl rode up on his horse. It was a massive Arabian and it kicked up rocks as he galloped past. Before Ember even realized what was happening, Daenerys bounded across the seat and then leapt from the truck.

The next thirty seconds played out like a bad movie. Labradoodle and Arabian engaged in what could have been described as either a death match or rough game of tag.

"Daenerys!" Ember screamed, realizing too late that the dog didn't even know her name yet so certainly wasn't going to respond while in a frenzy. Throwing all caution aside, Ember dodged the bucking horse to grab at Daenerys as she ran circles around him, dashing in to nip at the Arabian's legs when she saw an opening.

Thirty seconds was how long it took Carl, an expert rider, to regain control of his horse. Once he reined him in to a halt, Daenerys simply sat down and grinned at them all like it was a grand sport.

Mortified, Ember picked the dog up just as Bonnie came charging outside.

"What in the *world* is going on now?" she demanded, looking to her husband.

Using mostly expletives, Carl quickly described the "attack" as he jumped down from his horse. Daenerys had never actually touched him, but Carl still made a point of examining the legs of his mount.

"Dr. Burns, what kind of veterinarian brings an untrained dog to a client's house!" Bonnie yelled.

"I'm sorry," Ember offered. It was a weak apology, but it was all she had. Bonnie was right. It was inexcusable.

"No, I'm the one who's sorry," Bonnie continued. "You don't need to come back. If Butterscotch needs any further medical care, I know several vets that can take care of him without all the drama!"

Nodding in agreement, Ember turned away, still clutching the big dog in her arms. Staggering under the weight of one of the few friends she still had in Sanctuary, she slowly worked her way back to the truck.

SEVEN

Ember's house was the last one on a three-mile gravel road wrapping around Crystal Lake. It was named for its crystal-clear water, attributed to being glacier run-off from the highest peaks of the surrounding mountains. The gravel on the bottom of the lake was left behind ages before by a receding glacier, and it acted much like the gravel in a fishbowl, filtering the sediment.

Her twenty acres of land was mostly forested. Five acres were cleared and fenced, with the rambling farmhouse in the center of the clearing, but a majority of the fields were now overgrown, and the fencing in need of repair. Ember stood in the driveway for a moment, taking it all in. After growing up there, she was still awed by the raw beauty at their end of the valley. Beyond the fence line behind the house, the ground sloped upward, gently at first but then rapidly grew more extreme in angle. The countless ravines and ledges had been

Ember's playground, and she was looking forward to exploring them again.

Looking down at Daenerys, she had no doubt the dog would enjoy it, too. She wasn't mad at her for chasing the horse. It wasn't her fault that Ember put her in the situation in the first place. She should have never taken her back to Bonnie's. Daenerys was already having a hard day, between going to yet another new owner and being left alone several times. Yelling at her over something she obviously didn't know was wrong would only stress them both out.

"That relationship wasn't going anywhere good, anyway," Ember said to Daenerys.

The dog looked up at her with a longing she recognized as a need for approval. After reaching down to pet her sweet spot, Ember dropped to her knees. Daenerys's tail started thumping as they drew to eye level. Cupping her under the jaw, they stared at each other for a moment.

"I promise to take care of you and love you," Ember vowed. "All I ask is that you don't poop in the house."

Wiggling with barely contained excitement, Daenerys leaned forward and licked Ember once on the nose, as if to seal the agreement.

Laughing, Ember stood and patted at her thigh. "Come on! There's still enough light left to give you a quick tour of the main yard." Grabbing her purse, doctor bag, and dog supplies from the truck, she dumped it all on the large wrap-around porch before leading Daenerys around the side. She briefly debated putting the harness and leash on her but decided against it. The nearest neighbor was over a half-mile away. Ember believed that getting to know each other on their own terms was best.

In spite of being loose, the labradoodle stayed close, looking back constantly to make sure she knew where Ember was. It was a good sign.

"This is where Celeste lived," Ember announced, pointing at an old weather-beaten barn. Celeste had been a magnificent painted horse, perfect for the only sport Ember took part in: barrel racing. Sanctuary's one claim to fame was its annual rodeo. People came from all over the country to compete, and it was the town's largest source of tourism and revenue. And Ember was good at it. Well, used to be. When Celeste passed away Ember's senior year of high school, she swore she'd never own another horse. She'd been her best friend. It was the final factor in pushing her to accept the scholarship that ultimately led to her becoming a veterinarian.

Resting a hand on a top rail, Ember leaned against the fencing that encircled what used to be her training arena. It was where she'd gotten her first broken bone, hundreds of bruises, and the spirit of a competitor. She was acutely aware that the rodeo had already begun. It would culminate during the upcoming Fourth of July weekend with its main event the night of the centennial celebration. For the first time in a decade, Ember wanted to go. Maybe the old adage was right, and time *did* heal most wounds.

Her mother's cat chose that moment to leap onto the fence next to her, startling both Ember and Daenerys.

"Peaches!" she exclaimed, reaching for him, concerned that the dog might make a repeat performance with the much-smaller opponent. However, proving Becky right, Daenerys simply looked up happily at Peaches, tongue lolling. Encouraged, Ember let him go, and the two animals proceeded to sniff every available orifice before finally rubbing their faces together.

"Huh," Ember huffed, watching with amusement. She'd always told her mom she needed to change the cat's name. For one thing, it didn't sound like a boy's name. Second, the cat was black. Large, long-haired, and as black as midnight. But he liked peaches. Her mom found it hilarious. *Had* found it hilarious.

"I guess Peaches isn't such a bad name," Ember said softly when the cat turned his affections to her, rubbing in a circle around her leg. Her jeans soon took on a darker hue as the hairs stuck to it, and it reminded her that she still needed to get some laundry done and make dinner.

"Come on," she called to both of the animals. "Let's feed the chickens."

The only other boarders her mom left behind were a small flock of chickens. The pen was nestled in a far corner of the backyard, but she left the gate open during the day so they could free-range. It was important to put them in at night so the coyotes wouldn't get them. Her mom recently told her how bold they had gotten, and she found out the last couple of nights what she meant. They never used to come into the nearest pastures, but she woke up to one on the back patio a few nights ago. Hopefully, Daenerys would mark the property enough that they'd be a little more timid.

A few handfuls of feed brought the girls running, and once again, Daenerys proved herself a good farm dog by not chasing them off. Peaches, on the other hand, nearly pursued one into the woods.

Once they were back at the house, Ember watched the last of the light dance across Crystal Lake before it fell behind the tall mountains to the West, on the far side of Sanctuary. There was still over an hour until sunset, but the valley was blanketed in shadows long before then.

Although the air was still warm and heavy with the scents of summer in the mountains, Ember felt a chill. She didn't need the test results to draw her own conclusions. There was a murderer in Sanctuary.

EIGHT

Saturday morning greeted Ember with another sapphire-blue sky and a bald eagle's cry echoing over Crystal Lake. She woke with a fresh ambition to make the most of the day and to try and put anything negative behind her. She even selected a nicer pair of jeans after lingering over her favorite worn-down ones. While she planned on doing a lot of cleaning and moving furniture around, she also had a dinner date that night. Grabbing a generic T-shirt, she decided to look into having shirts made with the Sanctuary Animal Clinic name on it.

A short time later, as she was walking into the coffee shop next door to her building, she was reminded that she really should come up with a logo. Looking up at the wooden sign that bore the name "Nature's Brew of Sanctuary," she noted the stylish cedar tree carved to the far left, with one of its roots spelling out the store name. It was great marketing, and the tourists loved all the souvenirs inside with the same design on them.

"Ember!" Mel called out when she finally stepped inside. "What can I make for you?"

Ember smiled at the other woman, happy to see a familiar face. Since Mel lived below the store, it was convenient for her to work there on the weekends. That was why Ember hadn't seen her in there before, because she'd only been frequenting it since she took possession of the clinic that Monday before. However, Nature's Brew was rapidly becoming a staple to her mornings. In addition to their own specialty blend of coffee, they also served amazing pastries from a bakery in Refuge. Maybe they had cards she could pre-load and get a small savings. Or perhaps the owner had a pet. Bartering was still alive and well in Sanctuary.

"I'm going to be boring and get a simple tall vanilla latte. And pick out the most chocolate covered thing you have."

"Hot?" Mel asked.

"Yeah. I'll probably be back for something iced later on," Ember confessed. "I got hooked on coffee in college, and while I don't drink as much as I used to, I still rely on the afternoon boost."

"You don't have to explain your addiction to me," Mel laughed, preparing the drink. "I make bank on it." Two minutes later, she had the steaming drink and cream-filled, chocolate-covered doughnut on the counter for Ember. "So, umm, I heard you had some trouble last night?"

"Great," Ember moaned, handing cash to Mel. "Keep the change. So, tell me; how much damage is the rumor mill causing?"

Glancing at the two tourists in a far corner looking through postcards, Mel busied herself with wiping everything down while talking in low tones. "It could be worse. But Bonnie's pretty upset. Mrs. Jenkins is friends with Bonnie's best friend, and she was in here about an hour ago, talking it up like you caused the whole thing."

Pausing with the drink halfway to her mouth, Ember slowly set it back down. "What 'whole thing' would that be?" she asked evenly. The knot was back in her stomach.

"Well, according to her, you claimed the horse was responsible, and you drugged him to prove a false point. Then, when the autopsy revealed you were wrong, you went back out to her place and caused a scene all while trying to charge more for your services. But Ember," she rushed to add, her face a mask of concern, "while I want you to be aware of what people are saying, you also have to take it for what it is. Mrs. Jenkins is a known gossip, and I'm sure Bonnie wouldn't say all that. I doubt anyone would even be speculating if it weren't for you being the new vet. Especially with Doc Bernie's … past."

"The problem is that it really doesn't matter if she *did* say it," Ember replied, grimacing. "I know how rumors work. I grew up here, remember?" Taking a big bite of the doughnut, Ember tried to be reasonable and put it in perspective. "So long as this Mrs. Jenkins doesn't go out of her way to spread it, I might be able to still do some damage control."

"Umm," Mel muttered.

"How many?"

"Just one other person," Mel confessed. "Mrs. Jenkin's husband's boss's wife. They play cards on Friday nights," she added, as if it needed explanation.

Hanging her head, Ember took a deep breath. *Welcome back to the dark side of small town life,* she thought. "It's okay," she said firmly, looking back up at Mel. "Because one thing I've learned is that eventually the truth is revealed. The lab work and autopsy will be done in a few days, and hopefully Sheriff Walker will make some headway in finding whoever did this, if it is, in fact, a murder. I'll just have to work a little harder to repair my reputation. But I'm not going to validate any of those lies by defending myself to anyone."

Nodding in agreement, Mel glanced once more at the tourists and then lowered her voice further. "If it makes you feel any better, a whole lot more people are talking about the murder than they are about you and the horse," she whispered. "This is first time someone's been killed in Sanctuary in thirty years."

"We still don't know for sure how he died," Ember corrected. "Even though it would likely mean I'd take the brunt of even more scrutiny, I hope I'm wrong about the wound. That it's all just a tragic accident, and everyone can move on."

A jingling announced another customer before Ember could ask what Mel had meant by the reference to Doctor Bernie's past. Looking automatically toward the sound, Ember was greeted by another familiar face. One she hadn't seen in ten years.

"Mrs. Gomez!" she called out to her old high school English teacher.

"That's *Mayor* Gomez now," Mel corrected.

Mayor Gomez stared at Ember for a full five seconds before she broke out in a smile. "Ember Burns?" she asked, although it was obvious she recognized her. "I don't suppose you've changed much since I saw you last, but it *has* been quite some time!" Moving forward, the older woman reached out and grasped Ember's hand in a warm handshake.

Ember had fond memories of her teacher. Her senior year had some trying moments, and Mrs. Elly Gomez was a big supporter. She'd helped Ember complete her scholarship application and had written a glowing letter of recommendation.

"It's so good to see you!" Giving her hand an extra squeeze before letting go, Ember took in the changes the past years had made. While her dark hair was streaked with grey and the lines around her eyes were deeper, Mrs. Gomez had the same sparkling brown eyes and contagious smile. She was a small woman, barely coming past Ember's chin, but her personality was huge. It was no surprise that she'd managed to become the mayor of Sanctuary.

"I heard that Bernie's practice was finally purchased, but I didn't realize it was you until I talked with the sheriff this morning," Mayor Gomez explained, nodding at Mel to confirm she wanted her usual coffee. "I'm so sorry to hear of your mom's passing."

"Thank you," Ember replied, still unsure how to respond to people about it. Changing the subject was her favorite approach. "I have to say that I'm glad to be home. Although things have sure started out a bit rough," she added, figuring she'd get to the point first. It was obvious the mayor wanted to discuss it, since she already stated she'd talked to Walker about her.

"Poor Tom," Mayor Gomez choked out. Covering her mouth with a hand, she turned away for a moment to gather herself.

Mel and Ember glanced at each other, and Mel shrugged, also at a loss over the emotional response. Ember felt guilty yet again. Perhaps she *shouldn't* have brought it up.

When she turned back, the mayor dabbed at her eyes and tried to smile. "I'm sorry, it's just that I had both Tom and his wife, Vanessa, as students. I've kept in contact with them over the years, and recently Tom helped me out with my horse. It was such a shock to find out about his … passing, and I only just found out this morning that it might have been a homicide."

Ember was relieved to hear her say "might," and that she was speaking from information the sheriff gave her rather than rumors. "There's no need to apologize," she replied, placing a consoling hand on her shoulder. "We'll have more answers in a few days. It may still have been nothing more than an accident."

"I do hope you're right," Mayor Gomez answered while taking her finished drink from Mel. "There is, of course, never a good time for a tragedy such as this, but with the rodeo, centennial, and Fourth of July coming up, our town can't afford any bad publicity. I know that must sound horrible," she rushed to add when she saw the look on Ember's face, "but as the mayor, I also have to take these things into consideration. I'll be working damage control this week," she explained, glancing at the tourists now trying on sweatshirts, even though it would be over eighty that day. "The businesses of Sanctuary rely on the revenue from these events to carry them through the winter. It's part of my job to ensure the success of our summer season. Part of the appeal of our area is the lack of any violent crime, so I pray we can put poor Tom to rest without any fanfare, for *all* of our sakes."

Ember wasn't sure if the mayor meant it that way, but she looked pointedly at her when she said the last bit, giving the impression that Ember was a special part of the group needing a break. Shifting uncomfortably, she didn't know how to respond.

"Do you know what would be perfect?" the mayor chimed.

Surprised at her change in demeanor, Ember looked expectantly at Mayor Gomez. "No. What?"

"The parade committee is still in need of an Alumni Rodeo Queen!"

A deep flush spread rapidly across Ember's face. That was the *last* thing she expected to hear. Acutely aware of Mel's inquiring gaze, she avoided looking at her. "Oh, Mrs.—I mean, Mayor Gomez, I couldn't," Ember stuttered.

"But you *have* to!" she insisted, going so far as to take Ember's hand back in her own. "Our Rodeo Queen 2010 ended up moving this Spring, so we've been attempting to find a replacement ever since. You were 2008, right?"

Finally risking a glance at Mel, Ember was rewarded with a wide, mocking grin. "You were Miss Rodeo Queen 2008?"

Shaking her head miserably in response, Ember tried to think of a way—any way—to get out of it. "No. It was 2007."

The summer before her senior year, Ember competed in her last-ever barrel racing event at the famous Sanctuary Rodeo. She did well to place third in her class, considering the level of competitors the meet drew. The rodeo queen was selected by votes gathered locally in advance of the final Fourth-of-July parade. To be eligible, you had to be in a certain age range, a resident of Sanctuary, and entered in a qualifying event.

Ember didn't win the votes that year. Melissa Smart did. However, Melissa broke her leg during her race and was unable to ride in the parade, so the honors were transferred to the runner-up: Abigail Johnson. The night of the parade, Abigail must have eaten some bad fair food because she was found bent over a toilet fifteen-minutes before parade start time.

That was how the title of Miss Sanctuary Rodeo Queen 2007 was bestowed upon Ember Burns. By default. There simply weren't any other eligible girls left. She thought of the whole thing as a joke and never wore the iconic sash again after the embarrassing ride in the parade, but it was still hanging in her old room where her mother had kept it proudly displayed.

"Oh, that's right!" Mayor Gomez retorted, waving a hand. "2007. You must say yes, Ember! You can even ride my paint, if you'd like. She's a gentle horse."

"It'd be a great way to advertise the new clinic," Mel added. "You could have a banner made to drape on the horse."

Ember hung her head even further. It was a brilliant idea, and she didn't see any way out of it now. She felt a certain level of obligation to help, even though none of the mess with Tom and Butterscotch was actually her fault.

"Okay. Sure. I'd be happy to be your alumni in the parade," Ember muttered, unable to say the words "rodeo queen" out loud.

NINE

Ember nearly ran from the coffee shop, eager to retreat to her clinic and get lost in the manual labor of cleaning and sorting. She was still determined to keep a positive attitude.

"Who are you running from? And I can't tell if you're on the verge of laughter or tears."

Skidding to a stop, Ember discovered her Aunt Becky leaning against the front of her SUV. She hadn't even noticed the vehicle. Laughing, Ember balanced the doughnut on top of her coffee cup while digging the keys out of her back pocket.

"Both."

Following her inside without asking for an explanation, Becky knelt to give Daenerys a hug. "She's already graduated to free-reign of the place?" she asked, looking up at Ember.

"On a trial basis," Ember confirmed. "She's obviously a well-trained and behaved dog. Well, other than chasing horses and lending an interesting chapter to the story of my demise as a vet in the town of Sanctuary."

Standing, the grin faded from Becky's face. "So, you've heard."

"What Mrs. so-and-so said to someone else about what Bonnie said? Yeah. I heard." Grinning in spite of her tone, Ember set her things down and started opening a large box that contained a new file cabinet. "I plan on doing my best to give Butterscotch a clean bill of health, whether Bonnie wants my help or not. That's about all I *can* do, other than work to establish myself as a credible veterinarian. Which reminds me. Two people have now made reference to some sort of 'scandal' involving Doctor Bernie. Care to fill me in?"

Becky hesitated, looking down at her hands in a very uncharacteristic manner.

"Becky?" Ember pushed, her mild curiosity growing to one bordering on concern.

"Just before Christmas last year," Becky began without preamble, "Doc made a house call out at the Ellsworth Stables. You ever been out there?"

"No," Ember stated. "Mr. Ellsworth's daughter was a few years older than me and in a different 'class' of the elite. I may have competed against her once in barrel racing, but I never got an invite out to the ranch. Is it still a big deal around here?"

Nodding, Becky broke off a section of the forgotten doughnut and took a bite before continuing. "They've always been one of the wealthiest families in the county for as long as I can remember. Old blood, ya know? The roots run deep with the Ellsworths. High-class horse boarding, training, breeding, and stud service. Not to mention the largest herd of Angus in this part of the state."

"Stud service?" Ember questioned, frowning as she picked up her coffee. "Way out here in the middle of nowhere?"

Becky tossed a crumb to Daenerys, who was already sniffing around at her feet. "A few years back, the stables acquired a high-profile thoroughbred. I think he competed in the Kentucky Derby or something. Some of the big guns can bring in as much as two to three hundred thousand per 'service.'"

Choking on her coffee, Ember stared wide-eyed at her aunt. "You've *got* to be kidding!"

"Nope. Morton Ellsworth's horse wasn't nearly that valuable, but it was rumored that he charged a twenty thousand stud fee. So, when Doctor Bernie accidently killed him, it was a big deal."

"What?" Ember gave up on the coffee and set it aside again. As with any medical professional, causing the death of a patient was any doctor's worst nightmare. But causing the death of such a *valuable* horse would be a career-ender. "Wait a minute," she said slowly. "I thought that Doctor Bernie Chambers retired." She realized her tone was nearing accusatory, but the thought that her aunt may have misled her was shocking.

"He did, Ember!" Becky snapped back. "I would never lie to you. I have no idea what happened with any sort of malpractice suit that may or may not have been brought against him. That's all civil stuff, I believe. He had to have been insured, so I imagine Mr. Ellsworth walked away from it okay. But it was the one blemish on an otherwise wonderful forty-year-career, and I didn't think it had anything to do with you purchasing the building from him. I was going to tell you, of course, but it really didn't seem worth bringing up. I'll admit to not wanting to discourage you from moving back, but I could have never *fathomed* anything like this would happen."

"I'm sorry," Ember immediately offered. Her aunt was an honest woman, and it was obvious she only had Ember's best interest at heart. "I'm just a bit stressed about all of this."

"You're sorry; I'm sorry. Everybody is sorry," Becky replied without any heat behind the words. "The only reason it's a factor is because Bonnie opened her big mouth and made an issue about the tranquilizer you gave Butterscotch. Which is total BS, but I suppose in her distress over this, she's looking for a scapegoat. Since Doc Bernie admitted to dosing Ellsworth's horse incorrectly with a sedative, she's focusing on that parallel."

Ignoring the comment about Bonnie, Ember focused on her original question. "How did Doctor Bernie accomplish that?"

"Well, the horse had maimed itself by getting caught up in some barbed fencing. It was old stuff a farmhand left out instead of hauling off, and he was immediately fired over it. But the stud had a nice gash that became infected. Doctor Bernie was out there to administer some first aid and antibiotics, but that horse was having none of it. Apparently, when he drew the two medications, he mixed up the bottles and gave the poor thing a massive dose of sedatives in place of the antibiotic."

"That's horrible," Ember breathed. Knowing the history, Bonnie's behavior made more sense, but it didn't make her feel any better about it.

"The man is in his late seventies," Becky continued. "He should have retired some time ago, so it's not all that surprising it happened. It's just too bad it was something that led to the death of an animal in his care. Which reminds me..." Pulling an envelope out of her purse, she held it out to Ember.

"What's this?" Ember asked, unsure of the look her aunt was giving her.

"Payment for your services yesterday. And you don't have to worry about Bonnie letting you continue to care for Butterscotch, because I get to make that call now."

Taking the envelope, Ember tried to feel some sense of accomplishment about receiving her first official payment as a business owner. "Do I want to know how that came about?"

"The media showed up at the Hathaways last night, asking all sorts of questions, wanting to take pictures of their farm and the horse. It was the last straw for Carl. At this point, he doesn't care if the horse killed Tom or someone murdered him. He wants to distance himself from it all as much as possible. Since Butterscotch was still under the agreed-upon quarantine time, per our fostering contract, he can be returned. So, looks like I get my way in the end. He seems perfectly normal right now, but if you could swing by my place this afternoon and give him a checkup, I'd appreciate it."

Ember couldn't tell if Becky was happy with the arrangement or not. She knew it would be a source of stress between her and Paul, her husband. "Thanks, Becky. Of course, I'll go see him. Butterscotch is a sweet horse."

With a curt nod of her head, apparently signaling a change of subject, Becky joined Ember in pulling more furniture out of the boxes. "So, what had you running out of Nature's Brew like you'd kicked a beehive?"

"I ran into my old English-teacher-turned-mayor, Mrs. Gomez."

"Ah," Becky murmured. "Did she corner you into doing something in the parade?"

Ember grimaced and avoided eye contact. "Maybe."

"Oh, no, Ember. What in the world did you agree to?"

"It might possibly have to do with royalty." Placing her face in her hands, Ember waited for her aunt to put it together. It didn't take long.

Breaking out in loud laughter, Becky held her sides. "Shall I refer to you as 'My Queen' from now on?"

Daenerys picked up on the change in the atmosphere and began dancing around their feet, barking once to add her opinion.

Ember first gave Becky a crooked smile and then pointed a finger at the labradoodle. "*You* will be far away from that parade, my dear dog. It will be full of horses, and I don't feel like being in the middle of a stampede. And you," she continued, pointing at Becky, "only get to laugh at me *once*. Mel had the idea to carry a banner advertising the clinic, and it's actually a good plan. Plus, I don't think Mayor Gomez was going to take no for an answer."

"Well, you're definitely right about that," Becky agreed. Wiping at her eyes, she then surprised Ember by wrapping her in a big hug. "It's sure good to have you home, Em."

Stepping back, she clapped her hands together once. "Now! Put on a fresh pot of coffee. We've got some furniture to put together."

TEN

"Here, let me get that for you."

Ember hesitated behind the chair, unsure if Sean was serious. Sure enough, he walked around the small table in the back corner of the restaurant and pulled the wooden seat out for her. The Rusty Wagon Wheel was known for its killer barbeque ribs and steaks, not ambience. Failing to stifle a laugh, she sat and picked up the somewhat-sticky menu, watching him as he sat across from her.

He was even more handsome out of his doctor's jacket and in the relaxed setting. He had a day's worth of stubble growing, giving his features a bit more edge. Ember had always liked edge. His hands were a little too delicate and his physique not quite as robust as she was normally attracted to … but she found it hard to look away from his sharp, captivating eyes.

"So, what's it going to be?" he asked, raising an eyebrow. "Ribs, steak, or burger? I guess I should have asked if you're a meat-eater."

"I'm long past my vegetarian phase," Ember quipped. "I used to come here and get a hamburger every Friday night when I was a kid." Taking a moment to look around the inside of the cozy diner, she smiled at the variety of hand-carved wooden statues. There was likely one there for every year the Wheel had been open.

"We certainly don't want to mess with tradition." Sean took both of their menus and set them on the edge of the table before waving a waitress over. "Two of the Cowboy Blue burger baskets, and I'll have whatever dark beer you have on draft."

Ember fought the desire to change the order. She didn't actually care much for blue cheese, and wanted their basic cheeseburger. But part of the reason she accepted the invitation was to smooth things over with Sean, so in spite of finding him somewhat pretentious, she decided to ignore it.

"Just water with lemon for me, please."

"I heard you had some trouble out at the Hathaways?" Sean asked once the young waitress was walking away.

Grinding her teeth together, Ember carefully spread a napkin in her lap before answering. "Who hasn't heard?"

Snorting, Sean laced his hands together and set them on the table between them. "You and I both know you did nothing but help. How's the horse?"

With the topic of Bonnie apparently dismissed, Ember tried to stay focused. Sean was making that difficult, since he was leaning in and staring at her with an intensity that was overpowering.

"I … um, I mean … Butterscotch is good. He's fine. My Aunt Becky took him back in. I went out and examined him again this afternoon, and he isn't showing any sign of illness."

"Becky Stratton is your aunt? I didn't know that. It's good she's got the horse. Carl Hathaway didn't seem all that committed to him. And I've heard he's got a temper." Unwavering, he continued to hold her gaze.

Ember blinked a couple of times, resisting the urge to place her own hands over the top of his. She had the distinct impression that he knew *exactly* what sort of effect he was having. She squirmed slightly in the hard seat and was relieved when the server came back with the beer and water.

"You know, why don't you bring me a stout, too," Ember told her, taking the opportunity to shift her attention. "I've changed my mind."

Finally sitting back with the beer, Sean tilted his head to one side as he studied her. "All I know about you is that you're originally from Sanctuary. Do you have other family here besides Becky?"

"No. Just Becky and her husband and kids. My mom passed away last month. That's what brought me back. You?"

"I'm sorry about your mom, Ember. That's rough." He paused as the waitress set Ember's beer in front of her. "I was lured here five years ago by my wife. We met at school, and I'd just begun making some progress in my career at a large hospital in Seattle, when the position for the lead physician at the new clinic opened up. She grew up here, and I somehow let her talk me into the move. Our bliss lasted for nearly three years, until she left me to pursue her own dreams on the East Coast two years ago."

Unsure of how to respond to that, Ember took a long sip of beer. Doing some quick math, she figured he had to be between thirty-four and thirty-six years old. A list of questions popped into her head in regard to his ex-wife, but she held back. The dinner was simply the building of a foundation for a friendship. Nothing more. At least, not yet. Getting too personal might be a big mistake. She couldn't deny the chemistry between them, but she was holding back for the same reason. Chemistry had a way of being dangerous if not handled properly.

"Do you plan on staying in Sanctuary?" she finally asked, deciding to totally skip the whole ex-wife sand trap.

Hesitating just long enough for his disappointment at her lack of interest to register on his handsome features, Sean set his beer down and finally looked away from Ember. Message received.

"That all depends. I'm a final candidate at a hospital I've been trying to get on with for over a decade. If it falls through, I suppose I'll stick around."

"That must be exciting," Ember offered.

When he glanced up, he seemed to be weighing her attraction. This was where she could choose to either lean toward him and flirt back or remain distant.

Following instinct, Ember resisted his charm and, instead, took another long … very long, chug of beer.

His demeanor changed. It was hard to measure, but Ember suddenly felt like she was with Dr. Austin instead of Sean.

Was his ego really that sensitive? she wondered.

Their food came, and the rest of the dinner was filled with small talk and awkward gaps of silence. She was glad when they finished and she was able to say she needed to get back to the office, where Daenerys was waiting for her.

It wasn't until she stood to go and Sean moved smoothly behind her to help with the chair again that the spark between them was flamed further. He lingered mere inches from her and made no attempt to step aside and allow her passage.

Unable to fight the desire his nearness provoked, she turned slowly toward him and then looked up into his mesmerizing eyes. He was only a few inches taller, the gap between their faces less than a foot.

Her breath caught, and Ember was nearly lost in the moment as he closed the space by placing a hand at the small of her back and applying pressure.

The contact brought her to her senses. Bringing her hands up to his chest, she halted the motion. *Was he really going to kiss her?*

She hardly knew the man. Not that she was a prude, by any means; but at their age, Ember expected a certain level of courting to occur.

"Thank you for dinner," she breathed, taking a deliberate step back.

His face clouding, Sean abruptly removed his hand from her and widened the distance between them. "My pleasure. We'll have to do it again soon."

Ember wasn't sure what she thought of his personality. He seemed to be either seething with passion or ice-cold. But there was no denying her interest in wanting to get to know him more.

"I'd like that," she said warmly, reaching out to touch his hand lightly.

"Dr. Austin! Why haven't you returned my calls?"

Jumping at the piercing voice right next to her, Ember turned to find a rather large woman glaring at them both. Her long dark hair was in disarray, framing a pale face with large bags under her eyes. She stood with one hand on a generous hip, while the other clutched a huge to-go bag.

Sean coughed lightly once, clearly gathering his thoughts. "Dr. Burns, this is Vanessa *Clark*," he stated, emphasizing her last name.

Clark, Ember thought, trying to grasp the change in conversation. "Oh!" she gasped, realizing she must be the widow of Tom Clark. That would explain her appearance and red-rimmed eyes.

"Dr. Burns?" Vanessa repeated, her eyes narrowing. "Aren't you the busy-body that caused my Tom to get butchered?"

Ember recoiled, not understanding the accusation and wishing the woman would lower her voice. People at nearby tables were starting to turn their way.

"Mrs. Clark, I explained to you that the autopsy would have likely been necessary either way, and don't you want to know the truth as to how your husband died?" Sean was sounding very reasonable, but the distraught woman wasn't buying into it.

"There's no one in this world that would want to kill poor Tom!" she wailed, waving the bag of food in the air. The bottom was stained with grease, and Ember was afraid it might break loose.

So, the woman was blaming her for the autopsy. Ember recalled that Vanessa had been against it. How did Tom's wife even know that she was the one to find the suspicious wound? *Great.*

Glancing around the crowded room, she motioned toward the front door. "Why don't we go outside and talk?" Ember suggested. "I'd be happy to explain what I can."

"We don't need to go outside, and I don't need you to explain anything!" Vanessa continued. "The horse killed 'im! And now, thanks to you, I'm not going to be able to support my kids."

"What are you talking about?" Sean pressed, trying his best to lead her toward the exit. "Look, I know you're upset. You have every right to be." His voice was soothing, and Vanessa allowed him to take her arm and steer her along. "Tom was a good man, and I'm sure you're right. The autopsy is the only way to confirm that it was an accident. Like I told you earlier, we'll have those results back by Tuesday. There isn't anything else to be done until then."

Relieved to be out on the front porch, Ember walked awkwardly behind them. Now she *really* wanted to leave.

"You'd best be right," Vanessa lamented. "I just got off the phone with Tom's union representative. If he *was* murdered, I won't get a cent of his life insurance!"

Pointing at a newer, expensive-looking sedan parked nearby, she got more animated again. "How am I supposed to make that car payment? Or the mortgage? Or feed my kids?" she shouted, holding out the soggy bag of food. "When the sheriff talked to me yesterday, he said Tom was clearly trampled. *Clearly*, Dr. Austin!" She turned and wagged an accusatory finger at Ember. "It was going to be okay until you stepped in and fuddled everything up!"

Ember struggled to come up with a response. "I'm sorry," she eventually croaked out, but it was to the woman's retreating back.

ELEVEN

Ember jerked awake, springing up in her bed and blinking at the thick darkness. For a moment, she wasn't sure where she was, and then the past month's events came rushing back. The outline of her bedroom window came into focus, the curtains somewhat illuminated by a bright moon. It was her old bedroom. Home.

Her cell phone buzzed from its spot on the nightstand, casting its own blue light into the space before erupting with sound. The ring tone was a harsh one, meant to grab Ember's attention so she wouldn't miss a call. It worked.

Rubbing at her eyes, she snatched the phone up, worried that something was wrong with Becky or a member of her family. Who else would be calling in the middle of the night? Glancing down at the painfully bright screen, she saw that it was just past 2am, and it was an unknown caller.

"Hello?" Her voice was harsh. She didn't appreciate the scare for what was likely a wrong number.

"Is this Doctor Burns?" The man's voice was filled with urgency.

"Yes …" Ember answered, cautious. "I'm Doctor Burns. How did you get this number? Who is this?"

"I'm sorry to wake you, but I have an emergency with a foaling mare. Mrs. Stratton gave me your number. There isn't time for pleasantries, but I'm Morton Ellsworth. I understand you live at the Burns' place out on Crystal Lake? This mare doesn't have much time, Dr. Burns."

Jumping from the bed, Ember displaced Daenerys, who she didn't even notice was curled up alongside her legs. The dog had started out the night in her own bed on the floor but must have decided at some point to join her.

Pinching the phone between her chin and shoulder, Ember yanked on her blue jeans that had been cast onto the floor a few hours before.

"What's the problem?" Ember barked. It was rare for a foaling to have complications. About one in five hundred deliveries. But when there *was* an issue, it was often fatal for both the foal and the mare. Mr. Ellsworth was right; time was critical. Not bothering to change out of her over-sized T-shirt that passed for pajamas, she threw on a sweatshirt while holding the phone out.

"Water broke, but it's been over five minutes and there's still no presentation. Both my foreman and I think we feel a backend, so it has to be breech. At this point, I'm just hoping to save the mare. She's worth a lot. Are you able to handle that?"

Ember paused with one boot on. *Was she?* It was a valid question. This had the potential to be a very messy, hopeless situation.

Glancing at the clock in the foyer, she noted that two minutes had passed. "How far up Crystal Lane are you?"

"Not quite ten minutes. Entrance is on the South side of the road."

"I can be there in fifteen. Please have your foreman stay there. I might need the extra muscle. Do you have pulling straps? Mine are at the office in town." Ember had only ever watched the straps used once by the experienced veterinarian she shadowed during her internship. She delivered a few foals, but the one time they encountered a breech, she happily stepped aside. It didn't end well, as they often don't. But ready or not, Ember had committed to serving the community of Sanctuary, and if she wasn't willing to step up when called, then she had no business being a vet.

"Of course we have straps," Ellsworth retorted. "We're a professional stable, Dr. Burns. It's rare that we call upon anyone for outside services. Are you on your way yet? We're wasting time."

Ember's truck roared to life, and she watched the silhouette of Daenerys in the front window fade as she backed down the driveway. She'd tapped the speaker on her phone before setting it on the seat beside her. "Yes, Mr. Ellsworth, I'm already driving. I'll see you in a few minutes."

***

"Just cut the leg and pull the foal out! I won't lose this mare, Dr. Burns. She belongs to a high-profile client, and I can't afford the bad publicity right now."

Morton Ellsworth stood over Ember, his peppered hair framing an older but handsome face. As was common with men, the lines etched around his eyes lent character, and he held himself in a way only someone used to power could muster. This was a man accustomed to getting his way.

"*Publicity*?" Ember spat the word back at him with contempt.

Brushing past him, she yanked the leather pulling straps from the hands of the foreman standing behind Ellsworth. "The procedure you're suggesting is a drastic measure only taken when you have a dead breech foal, neither of which is the case here."

Quite often with a breech foal, the only way to save the life of the mare was to get the deceased foal out as quickly as possible. Though gruesome, the best way to accomplish that was to remove one of the foal's legs so that it could then be manually delivered. But Ember could feel the baby horse moving. It wasn't dead.

"We both felt its hind quarters when we examined her," Ellsworth insisted. Though he was still contradicting her, he made no move to prevent Ember from attaching the straps to the foal's legs.

"Perhaps, but its hind legs are both in the canal, and the mare's making some progress and moving it with the contractions. I'm certain it's a reverse presentation, not a breech. If we move fast enough, they can *both* be saved. Something I'm certain your client would be even more satisfied with," Ember added, looking up at the ranch owner.

When he only glared back, she made one last plea. She probably couldn't pull the foal out by herself. She would need the men's help. "I understand that you have a vast knowledge about horses, Mr. Ellsworth, and I appreciate that. However, you called me out here because neither of you is a veterinarian. I am. I'm asking you to trust my judgment here. And if that isn't enough, ask yourself why I've managed to get these straps on *both* of the foal's legs if it's breech?"

Morton Ellsworth paused, and then he turned to look at his foreman. Scratching at the stubble on his chin, he contemplated what she'd said. If he knew as much as he claimed, then he would understand that the major complication with a breech position was the legs getting caught up and the mare's inability to make any progress with moving it.

Without a word, the ranch owner waved a hand at his foreman, and the two of them stepped in behind Ember, each taking a strap.

Ten minutes later, a live foal was delivered, and Ember was done positioning it so its mother could clean it. It was uncertain as to whether it would survive. The next two or three days would determine its fate, but Ember was hopeful. There was no doubt it had suffered a lack of oxygen at some point, and it was impossible to know how severe it was. But the horse was already attempting to stand on its own and was responding to its mother's touch.

"When I'm wrong, I admit it."

Ember stood slowly and turned to face Ellsworth. Wiping her hands on a towel, she waited.

"I appreciate what you did here," he continued, gesturing to the two horses. "In spite of me. I have to confess that I had my reservations, given my history with your predecessor, but I'd say you've proven yourself tonight. I'll be giving you my endorsement, for what it's worth."

The fact that the man intended what he said as a compliment wasn't lost on Ember, but she'd had enough.

"My *predecessor*!" she nearly exploded. Throwing the towel down because it was the only thing available to her, she then balled her hands into fists and crossed them over her chest. "The good doctor, Bernie Chambers, is *not* my predecessor. I am in no way affiliated with him, have never worked with him, and did not buy his practice. I purchased a building and some of its contents. While I respect the time he put in here at Sanctuary, I'm sick of somehow being held accountable for whatever mistakes he made!"

Ellsworth took a step back from the barrage, but his demeanor hardened. "Whatever the case may be, Dr. Burns, whether it's right or wrong, people are going to make assumptions, and it would be in your best interest to take a compliment when you get one. Being so defensive only makes you look less professional."

Ember couldn't believe the man's arrogance, but the fact that he was right did nothing to placate her anger. The simple truth of the matter was that people had been questioning her abilities and comparing her to Dr. Chambers since she'd moved into the building. Lashing out at the one man to likely hold the most sway in the ranching community was career suicide.

Gritting her teeth, Ember forced the fire from her eyes. "Of course," she said softly. Intentionally relaxing her arms at her sides, she managed a small grin that she hoped didn't look like a grimace. "I apologize, Mr. Ellsworth. I'm tired, and it's been a very long couple of days."

Glancing at his watch, Ellsworth sighed heavily. "You're right. It's three thirty in the morning. We're both understandably irritable. We should perhaps get some rest, and then I'd be happy to set aside some time this week to meet with you and discuss our current veterinary needs. Regardless of what you think, I'd like to help harden the distinction between you and Dr. Chambers."

Her emotions made a hard swing from anger to embarrassment. One lesson Ember learned in that moment was that she first needed to work through her own feelings on the matter. The only true encounter she had with Dr. Chambers while he was a practicing vet was her senior year in high school when her horse, Celeste, fell ill.

The memory of that day came crashing down with such force that Ember closed her eyes against it, placing a hand to her forehead where a sudden headache blossomed. Normally suppressed, she found herself helpless against reliving that night.

It had been an unusually warm fall evening, and the crickets were just starting their chorus. Ember was leaning against the railing of the practice arena. Her mom led Dr. Chambers to the barn, where Ember knew poor Celeste was laying on her side, laboring to breathe. Whatever it was hit her hard and fast. The fifteen minutes or so that Ember waited felt like an eternity to the teen, and she wept while praying that the vet could save her horse.

When he finally came out, the answer was easy to read on his face. He placed a consoling hand on her shoulder and asked if she wanted to go tell Celeste goodbye. But she couldn't do it. The thought of looking into her best friend's big brown eyes one last time was too much. She cursed him and his inability to help her, before running into the woods. She came to understand that it wasn't his fault, of course, but she'd never forgiven herself for abandoning Celeste that night. She should have been there.

As her thoughts rushed back to the present, the anxiety she'd barely held at bay for the past month flourished with the intense emotions brought to the surface of her consciousness. Her breathing became ragged. Her mouth suddenly dry, she licked her lips before turning blindly toward where she thought she'd left her bag. She had to get out of there. But the movement induced a wave of dizziness, and she suddenly found herself down on one knee, the edges of her vision darkening.

TWELVE

The episode passed as quickly as it came, leaving Ember flustered and eager to convince Morton Ellsworth that she was okay. However, the stable owner insisted that he help her inside to his den, where he got her a glass of water. They both decided that some coffee would be a good idea before she attempted the fifteen-minute drive home on the dark winding road.

Sitting alone in the rich, mahogany-filled room, Ember sipped at the water and steadied herself. While Mr. Ellsworth was content with the explanation that she was physically exhausted from the big move over the past week and the late hour, Ember knew it went deeper than that. She wasn't eating enough, getting enough sleep, and was completely drained emotionally. She hadn't allowed herself time to heal from her mother's death, and it was bringing up old emotions.

Closing her eyes to ward off the onslaught she was afraid might follow, she was relieved when it didn't occur. Acknowledging her true emotions appeared to have taken the edge off.

Determined to take care of herself, Ember decided to take a day off from the clinic. It was Sunday, and by the time she got home and slept for a few hours, half the day would be gone anyway. Maybe she'd even go hiking. Now that she knew Mel would be helping her that next week, she didn't have any fear of not being ready for her grand opening the following Monday. Saturday was the Fourth of July and the centennial parade. She vowed to make the most of it.

Feeling much better, Ember set her glass down and tried out her legs. When she stood without any new dizziness, she began to pace around the outer edge of the sizeable den, studying the various pictures, sculptures, and knickknacks on display.

Pausing in front of what looked like an original Frederic Remington bronze statue of a cowboy on a bucking horse, Ember looked above it at a framed photo. In it was an adult version of Sandy, Morton Ellsworth's daughter. She figured it was at least five years old, since she didn't look much over twenty. Sandy was proudly posing next to a huge set of elk antlers, one hand resting on the impressive rack, the other holding a compound bow. Mounted above the photo was what Ember assumed was the same antlers. It had a plaque attached to it that read: *Sandy Ellsworth, First Place Finish, Washington Apple Compound Bow Competition, 2012.*

"Huh," Ember muttered, moving on to the next picture. It was similar to the first, but Sandy looked in her teens.

Just then, a set of headlights moved across the only window in the den, followed by the slam of a car door before it drove away. Feeling unreasonably guilty for her snooping, Ember moved back to her spot in the leather chair before whoever it was came inside.

Moments later, there was a noise at the front door. Several thumps and a giggle preceded the padding of shoeless feet coming toward the den. Ember waited.

Sure enough, Sandy finally stumbled past the arched entrance before stopping and taking an unsteady step backwards. Standing in the hallway with her purse in one hand and heels clasped in the other, she stood staring at Ember for several heartbeats.

As recognition slowly spread across her pretty, delicate features, she started pointing at Ember, causing the purse to fall to the floor. Ignoring it, she kept wagging a finger while trying to form the words she wanted to speak.

"I know youuu," she finally slurred. Pulling a band from her hair, she freed it, allowing the long blonde locks to cascade across her shoulders. "I know you," she repeated. "How do I know you?"

Sandy was obviously intoxicated and trying to sneak into the house like a teenager. Ember did her best to stifle a laugh. "I'm Ember."

Sandy continued to stare.

Ember sighed, bracing herself for the expected reaction. "Ember *Burns*."

"Oh!" Sandy gasped, clapping her hands together. "Yes! I remember now. Ember Burns so bright!"

Stopping herself from lashing out at the second Ellsworth that day, Ember only smiled. "Yup! That was one of the many endearing taunts I got to endure during my school career."

Missing the not-so-subtle innuendo, Sandy pointed again and leaned against the frame of the entryway, almost falling. "What are you doing here? My dad likes 'em young, but you're pushing it."

Blushing, Ember sat a bit straighter in the chair. "I'm a vet. I was called out for a foaling mare that was having a problem."

The other woman's features were transformed by concern, and she pushed herself back to a standing position. "The Queen's Hand?" Sandy blurted. "Is she okay?"

"She's going to be fine. The foal has a good chance of making it, too. It was a reverse presentation, but I … *we* were able to get him out."

Wiping a hand across her mouth, Sandy walked haltingly across the room to her father's large wooden desk. After pouring amber liquid from a glass decanter, she took a swig before turning back to Ember.

"Thank God. That would've been devastating if we'd lost The Queen. The mare's owner is our highest paying boarder. I don't know if the ranch would have survived that."

"I'm glad to have helped," Ember replied, picking the glass of water back up. While the stables certainly gave the impression of riches and success, it appeared that was not really the case.

"I've done a lot to stabilize things since taking over the finances," Sandy continued. "I don't know how Father survived the whole horse-killer fiasco, but things are still … delicate. Dad may be the best rancher in the state, but he's a horrible businessman. Although I keep insisting he overpays his staff, he refuses to listen to me. You'd think his farrier was using gold horseshoes!"

Ember felt that she should tell the intoxicated woman to stop talking, that she wasn't a personal friend of her fathers and shouldn't be hearing their private matters, but she had no clue how to go about it. Thankfully, Ellsworth chose that moment to return with a tray holding mugs and a fresh pot of coffee.

"Sandy!" he said, clearly surprised by her arrival. "I hope we didn't wake you."

Sandy set the glass down on his desk while shifting the hand holding her shoes behind her back. "No. I was just on my way up to bed, but I stopped to talk with your new vet. Ember and I knew each other in school, didn't we?" she asked, looking to Ember for confirmation.

"Yes, but Sandy was a couple of years ahead of me."

As Ellsworth crossed the room and set the tray down, he took in his daughter's clothing and appearance. His face clouding, he purposefully pushed the glass container of alcohol out of reach.

"Well, Sandy, if you were on your way to bed, don't let us keep you. It's awfully *late*."

Without responding, Sandy gave a nervous grin before brushing past her father. Ignoring Ember, she picked up her purse from the floor and left the room.

"I'm afraid I have to apologize for my daughter," Ellsworth stated, pouring a steaming cup of coffee and handing it to Ember. "She works hard and doesn't go out often. But when she does, it's usually to excess."

"No apologies needed," Ember rushed to say. The warm cup felt good in her hands, and as she took a sip, she hoped it wouldn't keep her up the rest of the night.

"She just returned home earlier this year, after going back to school and completing her business degree." Sitting down in an identical chair across from Ember, Ellsworth leaned back and crossed one leg on top of the other. "She's been a huge help to me."

After several minutes of polite conversation, Ember declined a second cup of coffee and excused herself. It was four in the morning, and she still needed to try to get some sleep.

"I'll call early this week to set up that meeting," Mr. Ellsworth promised as he walked her back out to the stalls to gather her belongings.

"That sounds good," she said sincerely, shaking his offered hand.

Walking away, Ember had mixed feelings about the whole encounter. While on the surface Morton Ellsworth and his stables looked nice and shiny, she had a suspicion that there were several darker layers underneath.

THIRTEEN

Ember woke at noon on Sunday to Daenerys licking her face. Convinced it couldn't be any later than eight in the morning, she rolled over and buried her face in the pillow. Undeterred, the labradoodle sat on her back.

"Daenerys!" The scolding came out as a muffled yelp that only further excited the dog. Her bladder unable to handle the pressure, Ember dragged herself out from under her friend and sat on the edge of the bed, blinking against the sunlight pouring in through the window.

Glancing down at her phone on the side table, she gasped. "Oh my gosh! Your bladder is probably about to explode, too. Come on!"

Feeling thrown off by the amount of time that had passed, and guilty about yelling at Daenerys,

Ember grabbed a dog treat on her way to the front door. "Here. Take this with you," she offered.

Daenerys smiled her doggy smile before gently taking the peace offering, and then she leapt through the front door and down the front steps. Running in circles like she'd been born and raised there, she then busied herself with sniffing multiple prime locations before finally relieving herself.

Ember laughed at the dog's antics and looked out beyond the driveway at Crystal Lake. It sparkled in the afternoon light, beckoning to her. Having already decided to skip the clinic that day, she contemplated their options.

No doubt, Daenerys would enjoy the water, but since it was so close, they could visit it whenever they wanted. Getting to Ember's favorite hiking trail, on the other hand, involved a twenty-minute drive east, into the mountains. She could make the hike itself as long or as short as she wanted, but she'd need to stop at the ranger station on the way to get a Northwest Forest Pass for parking at the trailhead. The federal parks should be open, even though it was a Sunday, since it was the peak of the camping season.

Deciding to go with the hike, she was tempted to grab her stuff and pick up a coffee on the way, but Ember forced herself to slow down and remember the resolution she'd made just eight hours earlier. Calling to Daenerys, she then went about making a large breakfast of eggs, bacon, and toast.

While eating that, she made and packed a large lunch to take on the hike, in addition to extra water and dog food for Daenerys. Digging around in the bag of goodies from Becky, she found a nice harness and leash. Dogs were allowed on the national forest trails, but they had to be leashed.

Tracking down her day hiking backpack was a separate issue, and she finally found it still in the trunk of her car in the garage. By the time everything was loaded in the truck, it was past one o'clock.

"We're fine," she assured Daenerys. "Still plenty of time. It won't be dark until around nine."

After shoving the pack behind the bench seat, she tugged one more time at the laces of her hiking shoes before climbing in next to the dog in the cab.

Following her road back to the head of the lake, she then turned onto a two-way highway that looped around the other side. It took them past the Ellsworth stables and up the increasingly steep terrain, the woods rapidly closing in and replacing the open fields.

It wasn't very far to the nearest federal park entrance. There was a small convenience store, restaurant, and ranger station that serviced the many campgrounds scattered for miles into the mountains. As Ember expected, it was a busy place. Not only was it summer, but it was also the weekend before the Fourth of July, the busiest time for campers.

"You get to stay here," she said to Daenerys. "I won't be long."

Outside the small office, positioned in between it and the restaurant, was an ice cream stand. Several kids and just as many adults were vying for a spot in line, and Ember was tempted to join them. But she could feel the time slipping away, so she headed inside the dim headquarters instead, a small bell announcing her arrival.

A young girl who couldn't have been more than nineteen or twenty was surrounded at a table by a large group of people decked out in brand-new hiking apparel. She had a map spread out and was attempting to explain something to them. By the looks on all of their faces, it didn't appear to be going well.

At the main counter, a middle-aged man and woman were engaged in some sort of disagreement with a parks employee.

"We have a reservation!" the woman wailed, slapping a hand down on the chest-high work surface. The man with her looked embarrassed but made no move to stop the display. "But our spot was occupied! We've got a carload of kids expecting to go camping, and I'm not about to go out there and tell them it's ruined because of *your* incompetence!"

The woman shifted her weight, giving Ember a peek at the man on the other end of the attack. He looked to be in his early thirties. He was standing across from the unhappy camper with his muscular arms folded across an expansive chest. Though most women might call him ruggedly handsome, Ember found his distinctive Native American features more intriguing than anything. He also looked thoroughly bored.

"Do you have your reservation number?"

"What?" the lady barked back.

"Your reservation number," the parks employee repeated evenly. "If you made a reservation, you would have been given a number, so as to avoid this type of conflict. Also, the campground you're referring to doesn't allow advance reservations. It's all on a first-come, first-serve basis. If you can show me your number, I can look it up and make sure you get to the right campground. Ma'am."

Ember stifled a laugh at the clever way he turned the situation around. He glanced up then, taking note that she was watching, but instead of looking annoyed, he gave her a small coy smile.

"Are you calling me a liar?" the lady blurted. Looking over at her husband, she placed her hands on her hips. "I think he's calling me a liar, Brad."

"Well, do you have the number?" Brad asked, finally growing a backbone. "All those places look the same and have crazy names. Maybe we *were* looking in the wrong one."

The woman guffawed but dug into her purse without saying anything further. Pulling out a piece of wadded-up paper, she then shoved it across the counter. The man took it and, after slowly pressing out the creases, tapped some keys on a computer hidden from view below the workspace. His face unreadable, he turned around and looked through a conglomerate of brochures in a rack on the wall. He came back with one and handed it to the woman.

"Here. This is the campground where you actually need to be looking. It's about ten miles in the *opposite* direction. Have fun, and please be sure to leave your camping spot cleaner than you found it."

A clear dismissal, the couple left without offering an apology, crowding past Ember and already talking about getting ice cream before they left.

"Busy day?" Ember asked, stepping forward.

"Just another day in paradise," the man quipped. "Where we save lives one-camper-at-a-time." He tapped a pencil against the counter with each word. "What emergency can I assist you with? Only, please don't tell me I've ruined your life too."

Laughing, Ember was impressed with his ability to bounce back so fast from the unpleasant encounter. "Nope! I'm easy. All I need is a Forestry Pass."

"Thank God," he breathed, pushing back from the counter. "*That* I am happy to help you with. I stopped by to give these guys a lunch break, and I somehow got roped into dealing with the rudest people of the day."

As he stepped away to locate the pass, Ember noticed he was wearing a park ranger uniform, complete with a badge and gun. No wonder he handled the couple so well.

"Where are you headed?" he asked when he returned. "And that'll be thirty-five dollars."

Handing him a credit card, Ember had a hard time not staring. He had amazing teeth. "Umm, the trailhead just past Parker Creek."

Nodding his head in approval, he rang up the transaction. "Smart. Even with all the traffic right now, that trail should be relatively quiet. It's not well-known. You must be from around here, but I don't remember ever seeing you before. And I would remember."

Blushing slightly at the compliment, Ember took the card back. "I grew up in Sanctuary, but I moved away ten years ago. I just came back recently. It's the first time I've been up here in years."

"I've worked here for two years now, and it hasn't changed much during that time. One of the nice things about working in a federal park that's protected."

"Are you Lakota?" Ember questioned, hoping she wasn't over-stepping. But he'd piqued her interest, and several of his features were familiar to her.

The man looked surprised for only a moment and then broke out in a wide smile. "Yup. Dakota Sioux tribe. But I have to say, that's kind of an odd question."

Her blush deepening, Ember rushed to explain. "My grandmother was a rebel back in her day and married a prominent member of a Lakota Blackfoot Sioux tribe. I haven't been back there to visit for a while now, but growing up, we would always spend part of our summer at their place in North Dakota."

Staring at her, a humorous twinkle in his dark eyes, he titled his head to the side questioningly. "So that would make you …"

"Around a quarter Lakota. I know, I know," she appeased, lifting up her ponytail. "I don't exactly look it, but I'm convinced that my mother's heritage is what saved me from the fate of fair skin and freckles."

Laughing, the man held out a hand. "I'm Nathan. Nice to meet you."

"Ember." Taking his hand, Ember didn't know if it was her imagination or not, but he seemed to linger before letting go.

A door at the back of the room banged open, and a young man in a parks employee shirt ran over. "Sorry, Nate. I mean, officer Sparks. I got a phone call, and then the restaurant took forever to make my sandwich. Thanks again for sitting in for me."

"Not a problem, Brandon. Happy to help out."

Standing there somewhat awkwardly, Ember watched the exchange. When Nathan looked back at her, she grinned and then pointed at the forestry pass still on the other side of the counter.

Snatching it up, he came around and held it out to her. "I'll walk you out," he offered.

Once they were outside, Ember was embarrassed to point out her rusty truck. "I inherited it from my mom," she explained as they walked toward it. She saw that his patrol car was only a few spots over. "She passed away about a month ago. That's what prompted me to move back home." She wasn't sure why she was telling him her life story, but she found it easy to talk to him for some reason.

"I'm sorry to hear that," he replied with the right amount of sincerity.

Glancing up at him, Ember realized that he was quite tall. His shiny black hair wasn't exactly long, but it wasn't cropped, either, coming to rest just above his collar. His angular features and high cheekbones could have made him look severe, but instead, she saw someone who was intelligent and friendly.

"Thanks. I'm working through it. Although this first week has started out with a bit of drama."

"I hope you weren't mixed up with Tom's death," he continued, his voice changing. "I haven't had a chance to talk with Sheriff Walker yet, but I know there's some question about what really happened."

"Not exactly," Ember answered, trying to figure out how to answer the question. "I'm a veterinarian. I was called out to the ranch initially because of the horse. I'm the one that … found him. Did you know Tom?"

Looking up at a rocky peak visible through the trees across from them, Nathan let out a long breath. "Yeah. We used to be friends. I met him the first winter I moved up here while out snowmobiling. Turned out we were both into riding."

"Horses?"

Laughing again, Nathan looked back down at her. "No. I've never really been into horses. Motocross. Tom and I have two-stroke bikes we like—liked to take to a track over in Parker. They have races in the summer on Saturday nights. Last year we went nearly every weekend, but I haven't seen him in close to six months." Pulling his wallet from his back pocket, Nathan took out a business card. "Here," he said while handing it to her. "My cell number is on there. You know, in case you need anything. Or a hiking partner."

Smiling, Ember took the card and stood tapping it against her lips as she watched him walk toward his patrol car. But as she turned to open the truck door, something he said made her pause.

Ignoring Daenerys's impatient bark, she called out to him. "Nathan!"

Stopping, he looked back at her expectantly.

"I'm just curious. You said you haven't seen Tom in almost six months. Why?"

"Well, up until January, his job as a farrier was hit-and-miss with the local clients. But then he got hired as a full-time hand and farrier at the Ellsworth Stables. I guess his time was suddenly too valuable to spend riding dirt bikes. Prior to that point, he never had anything good to say about the Ellsworth's. Funny how once that money was thrown his way, his opinion suddenly changed."

FOURTEEN

Ember couldn't get the thought out of her head. *"You'd think his farrier was using gold horseshoes!"* The drunken declaration made by Sandy Ellsworth that morning had taken on a whole new meaning.

Dodging a branch, Ember forced herself to slow down. The hike was supposed to be about relaxing, not to see how hard she could push it. Stopping in the middle of the groomed dirt trail, she put her hands on her hips and breathed heavily. The strong pine scent was soothing, and the warm air made it feel like it permeated everything.

The trail was steeper than she remembered. It was a good workout. Daenerys sat obediently at her feet, taking to the hiking experience like she'd done it all her life.

Unclipping the straw from the built-in camel pack, Ember took a long swallow of lukewarm water. Daenerys had just had a dip and drink from one of the many streams they crossed. She'd need a bath for sure when they got home. Smiling, Ember knelt down and gave the dog a hug.

"I'm glad you're here," she whispered into the silky fur of her friend's neck.

Yanking her head back unexpectedly, Daenerys whipped around to stare up the trail, back the way they'd come. Thrown off balance, Ember almost fell but caught herself and hopped to her feet. Though not growling a warning, the dog obviously heard something.

Her right hand hovering over the bear spray clipped to her waist, Ember breathed a sigh of relief when a young couple and black lab came into view. It was bear season, and there was a warning about recent sightings at the trailhead, in addition to a cougar.

"Hello!" Ember called out far in advance of passing. "My dog is leashed but is in training."

Stopping about ten feet away, the smart girl placed a hand on the top of the lab's head and waited to see how the two dogs reacted to each other. When all they did was wag and wiggle and whimper in earnest, wanting to play, they allowed the two to "introduce" themselves. After a solid two minutes of sniffing and then bouncing around each other, the three of them said goodbye and parted ways.

"Good girl," Ember praised. She scooped a treat from a convenient pouch built into her backpack strap and tossed it to Daenerys. She found it amazing how the two of them were already so comfortable with each other. It was a perfect match. Her Aunt Becky had always been good at pairing up animals to people.

Her Aunt Becky. That gave her an idea that might put to rest the feeling she couldn't shake about the income Tom was receiving for his work at the Ellsworth Stables. They were practically back at the trailhead, and she figured they might have cell reception. Digging her phone out, she was rewarded with a one-bar signal.

Ember paused first to sign out on a sheet located near the entrance to the trail. It was a way to help keep track of its use, as well as to locate the last-known location for a missing hiker. She was sure to sign in and out, especially if hiking by herself.

She dialed her aunt's number and then slowly undid the clasps on her pack. She was already starting to stiffen up and would, no doubt, be sore later.

"Hey, Ember! What's up?"

Smiling at the ever-present energy in her aunt's voice, Ember sat her pack down and started feeling around for the truck keys with one hand. "Not a whole lot, Becky. I took Daenerys up to the Parker Creek Trail. She did fantastic!"

"I had a feeling she would."

"Yeah. You were right, as usual."

"What did Morton Ellsworth want last night?" Becky questioned. "I hope it was okay to give him your number. He sounded desperate."

"That's sort of the reason I called. I want to ask you a question about Tom. I went out to the Ellsworth Stables this morning for an issue with a foaling mare and ended up having a rather interesting conversation with Sandy."

"Sandy Ellsworth?" Becky questioned. "I knew she came back from the great beyond earlier this year, but I haven't actually seen her. That was brave of you to go out there, Ember. Brave or stupid. Depends on how it went."

Laughing, Ember had to agree. "You're absolutely right, and it was almost catastrophic. But it turned out okay in the end. Both the foal and mare survived, so far, and I have a meeting with Morton Ellsworth later this week to 'go over my potential future.'"

"With a man like Morton backing you, Ember, that might be just the break you need right now. Please don't tell me you're going to do something to mess it up. Why in the world would you have been having a conversation with his daughter about Tom?"

"I didn't know at the time that it was about Tom," Ember rushed to explain. "Mr. Ellsworth was getting coffee when Sandy literally stumbled by. She was quite drunk. Said some things about the stable's finances that she shouldn't have, including that her father insisted on paying the farrier way too much. I just found out inadvertently, a few hours ago, that Tom was that farrier. Guess he got hired back in January to replace the guy fired for getting the horse hurt."

"And?" Becky said slowly, obviously not seeing the connection.

"Becky, do you know how much the garage cost that Paul was going to build for Tom?"

"Of course I do," Becky confirmed. "I'm the bookkeeper for our business. It wasn't anything too extravagant, but it was big. Three-car bay, plus a shop area and office space above. Tom said something about opening his own farrier business. It came to just under thirty-five thousand."

Whistling, Ember stood up with the keys in hand. "That's a good chunk. How was Tom going to pay for that?"

"I don't know. Never got that far." Becky paused. "But you know what? Hang on a sec and let me go ask Paul. I know he and Tom talked just a few days before he died."

Ember busied herself with getting her gear and Daenerys in the truck. Although it was almost five, there were still three other cars parked at the trailhead. While no one was visible, she'd rather continue the conversation inside the truck, out of the open. She was just settling into the driver's seat when Becky came back on the line.

"Just as I thought, Tom signed the final papers last week. He was supposed to come by this next week to give a ten-thousand-dollar deposit. And—"

"And?" Ember prompted when Becky hesitated.

"He claimed he was going to pay the balance off with cash, once the project was completed."

"Becky, you know as well as I do that a farrier in this state is lucky to make twenty-five to thirty thousand a year, working full-time. And didn't he get a new car a couple of months ago? Was no one curious as to where all this cash came from?"

"Honestly, Ember, it wasn't anyone's business where he was getting his money from. I assumed, until just now, that he was getting a loan for the garage. Paul was planning on talking to me about it because he was skeptical, but then he let it go after Tom's death because he didn't think it relevant anymore. What are you thinking?"

Picking at a thread on her hiking slacks, Ember wondered the same thing. She wasn't sure, but something wasn't right; and it all seemed to lead back to the death of the horse that last December.

"It's probably nothing, Aunt Becky," she said aloud, not sure how to explain it. "I'll give you a call later. I need to come by and check on Butterscotch again."

"Sure, Ember. Anytime. I'll talk with ya later!"

Slowly lowering the phone, Ember stared out at the evergreens for a minute. Making up her mind, she started the truck. "I guess we're going by the clinic today after all," she told Daenerys.

When moving things around the other day, she'd discovered a back room that contained what appeared to be all of Doctor Bernie's patient records. There was one in particular she was interested in.

It was time to find out what made that horse so special.

***

"Black Shadow's behavior rapidly deteriorated, with his agitation increasing until he was exhibiting all the symptoms of morphine excitement." Ember lowered the paper and stared at Daenerys resting on her feet. "Morphine excitement?"

The dog lifted her ears but not her head. She was beat from the long hike.

They were sitting on the floor in the back room of the clinic, papers scattered around them. Several stacks of cardboard boxes lined one wall, and the only furniture was an old table on the opposite wall with a lamp on it. Ember had removed ten boxes and restacked them next to her before finding the one containing the E's in it. Apparently, Dr. Bernie Chambers didn't upgrade his filing system at any point during his forty years of practice. It was a mess to wade through.

The Ellsworth file was one of the thickest she'd seen, but the report in her hand was the last one in it. It was a detailed account of that fateful encounter just over six months prior. Based on other exam notes, the thoroughbred, Black Shadow, was a stallion in his prime. The original remarks regarding the injury from the barbed wire were unremarkable. It sounded like a typical gash that was expected to heal without complications. Even when it became infected, it should have still been a simple procedure. Reading what happened, it was anything but ordinary.

Ember was familiar with the use of morphine for pain control in animals, but the settings she'd used it in were different from what transpired with Black Shadow. For surgery, the animals she worked on were given a cocktail of drugs intravenously. Morphine was one of many differing levels of opioids, and the clinic she worked in opted for a cheaper, less-potent version. In the field, they often turned to tranquilizers to calm the animals during procedures, which was a totally different class of drug, with varying doses and effects. Still, she was educated in the basic doses for injection, and it was obvious what had happened with the expensive thoroughbred.

Dr. Chambers was giving him two medications: IV antibiotics and an injectable pain killer, morphine. The amount drawn up in the syringe for the antibiotic was about four times that of the morphine, so when he somehow got the two mixed up, he essentially overdosed the horse, eventually causing its central nervous system to shut down. When the horse became agitated and then had a seizure before he stopped breathing, it wasn't clear at the time if it was an allergic reaction to the antibiotic or something else. At that point, Dr. Chambers didn't think he had even administered the morphine yet.

Shaking her head, Ember set the four sheets of paper out on the floor in front of her. The veterinarian didn't take long to figure out what he'd done. Although the bottles of medication didn't look all that similar, he somehow confused them. It was late, he was tired, and the lighting in the barn was dim. She could imagine his horror when he pieced it all together.

Grabbing her phone, Ember did a search for "morphine excitement in horses." After skimming through the information, she had a better understanding of what happened. She wasn't familiar with the term because it only occurred when morphine was given intravenously, which she would never do. In the horse world, intravenous was different than with humans. It didn't necessarily mean a bag of fluids was hung up on a pole with a tube. It simply meant that the drug was administered directly into a major vein in the horse's neck, versus the muscle. It was a risky procedure with *any* medication, if not done by a licensed vet who knew what they were doing.

Excitement.

"Oh my gosh!" Ember exclaimed suddenly. "Butterscotch!"

Daenerys had fallen sound asleep and leapt to her feet when Ember yelled. The space around them was limited, and the labradoodle fell into a box at the bottom of a precarious stack. Before Ember could react, it toppled over, scattering files and loose papers everywhere.

Daenerys gave a small yelp and jumped back the other direction, into Ember's lap, causing them both to fall over to the side.

Laughing, Ember sat up slowly, holding Daenerys close. "It's okay!" she cooed, petting the soft curls of her head. "But I think I know what was wrong with Butterscotch," she continued, looking back at the pages still visible under the avalanche of other documents.

Reaching around Daenerys to gather them up, she lingered over the one titled "Necropsy Report," which was the animal equivalent of an autopsy. Skimming over the information it contained, she saw that the toxicology was positive for excessive amounts of opioids. A red stamp of "official copy" was inked across its middle.

A second sheet stapled behind it was an exact duplicate of the report and was obviously the original. Except that a small swath of content near the bottom was blacked out with a marker. Flipping back to the "official copy" document, she confirmed that the lower portion was filled in with only four words: normal and within limits. It was the fertility section. The original had two or three sentences and Ember would bet it was a more detailed report of the horse's sperm count.

"That would have been important for a twenty-thousand-dollar-a-date stud horse,"Ember mumbled.

Slipping the papers into her leather bag, she then stood and looked down at the chaos she'd created. It was close to seven, and she hadn't had dinner yet. Turning off the light and calling to Daenerys, Ember made the decision to leave the filing to Mel. She also decided to make two phone calls in the morning. One would be to the previous office worker, Marissa Thomas. She'd left an open invitation to Ember for afternoon tea, and she had a feeling the older woman might be the best way to get some answers. Her other call would be to the lab.

"I've been going about this whole thing the wrong way," Ember explained to Daenerys as they made their way to the front door, turning off lights as they went. "I think Butterscotch was framed, and I'll bet you a tox screen will show that there was morphine in his bloodstream."

Ember was hoping the lab would be able to add the other test onto the already existing order. She didn't see why not. The blood she sent should still be there, refrigerated.

"Dang it!" Stopping at the front counter to get her keys, she pounded a fist on the surface in frustration. Ember was worried that Bonnie may have been right after all. At least to the extent that she didn't do her job very well. She should have thought to check for drugs before. It was a quick test and may have been done by Friday night.

"Come on," she called, leading the way outside.

The evening air was just starting to cool off, and the shadows were gathering. Ember strode to her truck with a new determination. She was more certain than ever that there *was* a killer in Sanctuary, and she was going to figure out who it was!

FIFTEEN

The historic farmhouse was like a scene ripped from a book. A long gravel driveway was lined with white elm trees and led to a classic two-story, gabled house. Ducks ran across the parking area toward a picturesque pond, complete with a small dock and rowboat. There were several acres of cleared land and grass, which stood in contrast to the surrounding woods and steep mountains.

A teenage boy was in the distance on a riding lawnmower, likely a neighbor. Ember would have to get his name before she left. She'd need some help maintaining her own property, and it turned out that Marissa lived right down the road from her.

When she'd called Marissa Thomas that morning, she didn't think the woman was going to honor her original invitation. Granted, it had been several weeks since they'd spoken and it was perhaps extended as a courtesy, but Ember didn't care. She honestly wasn't concerned if she came across as pushy or socially inept. She needed some answers, and Marissa seemed like a good place to start. After an obvious pause, Marissa said Ember would be welcome to swing by after lunch for tea.

Ember called the lab first thing that morning and confirmed they could add on the toxicology test, then she and Mel finished getting the rest of the furniture unboxed. A twinge of guilt tugged at her as she thought about the state she left the younger woman in a few minutes ago, but she didn't plan on being gone for long. Anyway, Daenerys would keep her company.

Her confidence ebbed as she got out of the truck, and Ember gave herself a small pep talk on the way up the broad steps. *She's the only one that might know the truth about that horse.*

After reaching out to bang the ornate brass knocker, she stuck her hands in her pockets. *She isn't going to bite.*

The heavy wooden door swung open, revealing a short, rather plump woman in her late sixties. Her grey hair was pulled back in a tight bun, her thin lips drawn into a line that resembled a grimace. She didn't appear to have fangs, but the rest of Ember's poise dissipated.

"I'm, um …" she stumbled over her words. "I'm Doctor Ember Burns."

When Marissa failed to extend a welcome, she tried again. "We spoke on the phone this morning.

Do I have the wrong house?" They had never actually met in person, and Ember began to wonder if maybe it really *was* the wrong house.

"Dr. Burns. It's nice to finally meet. You've got the right place. I'm Marissa Thomas. The tea is ready if you'd like to come inside."

Ember was having a hard time reading her. While what she said was pleasant enough, *how* she said it wasn't very inviting. But the older woman took a step back and gestured for her to enter.

Smiling, she stepped past her and discovered the house to be just as conflicted as its owner. While the rough-hewn wooden floors and open beam ceilings were everything country, the décor was in direct juxtaposition. The furniture in the sitting room Marissa led her to was all sharp angles and white, grey, and cream colors, versus the wood, leather, and warmer colors you'd expect. An ornate oriental rug covered most of the floor, and a very modernistic metal chandelier hung in the middle of it all. The one contrast was an antique wood gun cabinet tucked into a corner, filled with expensive-looking hunting rifles.

"It was my late husband's," Marissa explained. "I don't hunt and never enjoyed shooting, but there are some things that you simply must let be."

When Ember turned back, she found Marissa staring intently at her and had the distinct feeling she wasn't just talking about the cabinet.

Simply nodding in agreement, Ember sat down on a very Victorian chair in the central sitting area.

There was a nice tea set already put out on the coffee table. Marissa must have seen her coming up the driveway.

"How are you settling in?" Marissa asked, sitting down opposite her. "Are you finding everything okay?"

"Mel and I have made some progress," Ember replied. She noticed a nice light lilac scent and then spotted some fresh-cut branches in a vase. Her mother had a giant purple-flowered lilac tree in the backyard. The scent was synonymous to summer, growing up. She'd have to remember to check and see if it was still blooming.

"Doctor?" Marissa repeated. "I asked when you're opening."

"Oh! Sorry, the official day is next Monday. Though, I've already had a couple of clients."

"So I've heard." The contempt in her voice was clear. "Do tell me, Dr. Burns, what it is that brings you out here today? Because I doubt it's to discuss furniture and drink tea."

Ember cleared her throat. She realized she hadn't even poured a cup of the tea. *Smooth, Burns,* she thought while reaching for the kettle. *That's why I'm a veterinarian and not a cop.* "Please, call me Ember."

"I'm from a more formal era, *Doctor* Burns," Marissa stated. Taking the pot from her, she also poured a steaming cup and then settled into the high-backed chair.

Ember decided getting straight to the point would be her best move. "I came across some papers that I hoped you might be able to give me some insight on."

Eyes narrowing, Marissa took a small, slow sip before answering. "And what papers might those be?"

Shifting uncomfortably, Ember reached for a cookie set out on a plate alongside the tea. "The necropsy report for Black Shadow."

Pausing with the teacup poised just below her lips, Marissa made no attempt to hide her disdain. Eyes widening, her nostrils flared. "What right do you have to be digging around in Dr. Chambers's records?"

Trying not to feel overly deflated by the response, Ember struggled to find the right words. "The doctor left everything there for me to help make the transition easier. While I'm not technically taking over his practice, he expects most of his patients will transfer to me."

"I know that," Marissa spat. "But that doesn't explain why you're snooping in *that* file! The man is retired. He paid his penance. He doesn't need his name dragged around in the mud anymore."

Realizing the older woman was reacting out of loyalty to her friend rather than simply being spiteful, Ember relaxed a little. *That* she could work with. "I have no intention of dragging anyone's name around," she said with sincerity. "I was called out to Ellsworth Stables a couple of nights ago, and the encounter led to me wanting to find out some more information about what happened with Black Shadow."

"Unless that was the horse you got called out there for, then you still don't have a legitimate reason to be looking into it."

Ember tried not to squirm under the woman's judgmental stare. "You know privacy laws don't extend to animals."

"I didn't say it was illegal. We're talking about ethics here, Dr. Burns."

"Ethics?" Ember exploded with more venom than she intended, causing Marissa to flinch. "A man is *dead*, Mrs. Thomas. I don't give a crap if you think it unethical for me to look into the file of a dead horse!"

"Wait a minute." Marissa put a hand out in a "stop" gesture. "You're talking about Tom Clark. What on earth does that man's death have to do with Black Shadow?"

With the question laid out, Ember came to the realization that she didn't know how to answer. That's why she was there. Maybe simply stating the facts would be the best approach. "Did you know that Tom was working there? At the Ellsworth Stables."

"Tom working for Morton? No way. That would never happen."

"He was hired as his new lead ranch hand and farrier in January sometime and was paid very well, according to Sandy Ellsworth."

Marissa was speechless for a moment. Gathering herself, she took several sips of tea before answering. "Tom never had a good thing to say about Mr. Ellsworth. I hadn't seen him since the practice closed. And I don't have any horses anymore, so I've had no reason to speak with him. I know people change and he was hard-up for cash, but it's still hard to believe."

"Well, something changed right around the same time Black Shadow died," Ember urged. "And he was being paid enough to afford a new car and build a garage."

"What are you implying?" Marissa demanded, her demeanor solidifying again.

Ember felt like she was playing a game of cat-and-mouse. And the mouse had just dodged back out of reach again.

"What was blacked out on the necropsy report?"

Marissa paled. "You found the *original*?"

"Yes." Ember continued without preamble. "And the fertility section had been filled out. Differently, I'm sure, then what was on the final, official document."

"That senile old fool," Marissa muttered, gathering all of the china back onto the tray. "What it said is of no consequence to you and has nothing to do with what you *think* Tom got himself involved in." Turning with the tray toward the front hall, it was a clear dismissal.

"I would imagine," Ember pushed, "that if the insurance company found out the prized stallion was

… say, *infertile*, it would be hesitant to pay out the policy."

Shoulders sagging, Marissa stopped but didn't turn back around. "Let this go, Dr. Burns. Bernie was diagnosed with early dementia last year and should have retired long before the accident happened. Certain … agreements were made to keep any potential lawsuits from escalating. The outcome worked out best for all involved. You can see your way out."

Watching the woman walk slowly from the room, Ember was left with more questions than when she'd gotten there.

SIXTEEN

"The first thing we should do is set up a Facebook page for the clinic," Mel declared. "I'm working on the logo, and tomorrow I'll go to the sign shop to see what they can have made up for you. And you do realize that I'm totally going all geek on you with the decorations in this room, right? I'm talking a R2-D2 garbage can and Phaser drawer knobs."

Ember and Mel were sitting in the new break room. Mel explained that morning that it used to be Marissa's office, and she refused to take it over as her own. Bad juju, or something. Instead, she settled for a smaller room that was an old furniture graveyard. After clearing it out, they'd been amazed at how much usable space there was. It even had a window.

"Ember, are you listening? Hello! Earth to Ember!"

"Sorry," Ember laughed. "I'm still mulling over my disastrous encounter with Mrs. Thomas."

"Pffft." Mel pursed her lips. "That old cow doesn't like anyone. She's never said more than two words to me at a time. I warned you."

"Yeah, but when you said 'not very friendly,' I don't think you did her justice."

"At least you learned that Doc Bernie has dementia," Mel said, her voice softening. "That explains a lot. I knew he wasn't acting the same, but he never confided in me. For whatever reason, Marissa was good friends with him and his wife."

"I'm sure she isn't all that bad," Ember countered. "I think she's trying to protect her old friend. She essentially confirmed the stallion was sterile, without actually saying it."

"So, you have no proof," Mel pointed out. "That blacked-out paper is worthless. Even so," she continued, crossing her arms, "I might have to agree with Marissa on this one."

Ember studied Mel, raising her eyebrows in curiosity.

"Let's say Black Shadow *was* sterile, and Doc Bernie's mistake ended up saving Ellsworth money in the long run because of the insurance plan." Mel sat up a little straighter on the loveseat, the only original piece of furniture left in the breakroom. Leaning toward Ember, she ticked off the points on her fingers. "Omitting that finding from the necropsy report prevented the Doc from getting sued. Revealing that now would only get Doctor Bernie in trouble for fraud and open the doorway for Ellsworth to then sue him, *and* I really don't see how any of it has to do with Tom's murder!"

Before Ember could counter Mel's very reasonable observations, her cell phone began to ring. Glancing at the caller ID, a small thrill coursed through her. It was the lab.

"This is Dr. Burns."

"Dr. Burns. Gary over at Quick Quality Labs. I've just sent you an email, but I wanted to give you a call since it's nearing the end of the day and I know you're anxious to get the results."

"Thank you, Gary. I appreciate it. What's the news?"

"Mixed. The results for bacterial and viral agents is negative. However, the toxicology turned up a hit for opioids. Barely above trace amounts, but it could back up your suspicion for morphine."

"Right. Okay … Thanks for the call."

Slowly lowering the phone, Ember's mind was spinning with the implications. As it all tumbled around, a random thought crashed through. Eyes widening, she looked up sharply at Mel. "What if," she said evenly, "Morton Ellsworth *knew* his prize stallion was sterile?"

***

"Ember, I sure hope you have some proof behind an accusation like that." Sheriff Walker stood with his thick arms crossed over his chest. The scowl on his face was so deep that the confidence Ember felt moments earlier, as she walked in the front door of the station, quickly faded.

"It's not so much an accusation as a suggestion to a possibility." Even as she said it, Ember knew it sounded lame.

Glancing over at Sean, she wished that the doctor wasn't there. She didn't know why he was at the sheriff's office, but she didn't think to ask him to leave when she found him sitting and talking with Walker. He hadn't called or texted her since their dinner Saturday night. Whether it was because he wasn't interested or that he was waiting a customary amount of time, she wasn't sure. Either way, it added to the awkwardness of the situation.

For whatever reason, listing out her suspected chain of events to the sheriff didn't come off sounding as convincing as it did when she said it to Mel. "I can go get you the necropsy report if you want to see it," she offered.

"I don't need to see anything," Walker quickly answered, waving one large hand in the air as if batting down her suggestion. "Morton Ellsworth is a prominent businessman in Sanctuary, as well as a friend. And he certainly didn't conspire with Doctor Chambers to kill off his horse!"

Ember flinched as the sheriff's voice rose, and she suddenly felt a few inches tall. "But what about Tom?"

"What *about* Tom? You think I don't know he worked for Morton? I've already talked with him about his employee, Ember. It's what law enforcement does during an investigation."

"Ben," Sean interjected. Standing, he made his way toward the office door as he spoke. "You can't fault Ember for looking for answers. Those opioids got into Butterscotch's bloodstream somehow, and while it's likely a coincidence that he possibly suffered the same, although less significant, reaction that Black Shadow had, it might still bear consideration."

When Ben Walker turned his steely gaze on him, Sean lifted his hands in defense. "All I'm saying is that I can follow her reasoning. Look," he continued, addressing Ember, "I've built a rapport with Vanessa Clark. If you like, I can ask her about the money. Find out how Tom was really planning on paying for that garage. Maybe there's a simple explanation."

Relieved that someone was finally listening to her, Ember smiled at him gratefully. "Thanks, Sean. I appreciate it."

"Should I just go ahead and deputize both of you now?" Sheriff Walker barked. When neither of them responded, he ran a hand over his head and let out a moan. "Fine. I can't tell you who you can or can't talk to. But for what it's worth, Ember, even if

Black Shadow *was* sterile and Tom caught onto it somehow and used the information to get himself a nice-paying job, that's hardly a motive for murder. But while it's insufficient to explain his death, it *would* be enough to critically damage the reputation of Ellsworth Stables, so be careful who you say it to. You of all people should know what a rumor can do."

Blushing a deep crimson, Ember was aware of Sean waving a silent goodbye and then found herself alone with the sheriff. "That's why I'm here, talking to you about it," she stated. "I don't plan on sharing it with anyone else, but I wanted you to at least have the information and the test results. But I should have waited for Sean to leave."

"Sean is fine," Walker huffed, waving his hand again and sitting behind his desk. "He's discreet. Comes with being a doctor. He was actually here delivering the news that my cholesterol is sky-high, so it looks like I'll be cancelling my reservations at the Rusty Wagon Wheel."

The mention of the restaurant reminded Ember once more of her dinner with Sean, and she wondered if they'd ever get a chance to try again under more normal circumstances.

Normal, Ember thought wistfully. She was beginning to forget what that was.

SEVENTEEN

It was still dark when Ember drove down her road toward the clinic Tuesday morning. It was ridiculously early. After staying up most of the night Saturday and sleeping half the day Sunday, her schedule was off. As a result, she wasn't tired by her normal bedtime Sunday, but she had to be up early to meet Mel Monday morning. By Monday night, she was dead-tired. Especially after her exchange with Sheriff Walker. She'd found herself nodding off on the couch with a TV dinner still in her lap.

Daenerys woke her up before four to go outside, and she wasn't able to fall back asleep. When she started craving a cup of coffee and found herself making a pot at four fifteen, she gave up and got dressed. Normally not a morning person, she decided to take advantage of it and get a head start on the day. She was planning on spending some time with Butterscotch that afternoon and was feeling guilty about leaving Mel alone yet again. She could make up for it by getting a bunch of things checked off the list before Mel even got there.

"Mel will be babysitting you again today," Ember told Daenerys.

Lifting her head from the seat of the truck, the dog tilted it to one side and gave what looked suspiciously like a real smile. Ember suspected a lot of treats disappeared from the display rack when she wasn't around.

It wasn't yet five when they pulled in front of the clinic, and the sky was just beginning to brighten to the east. For a moment she wished she'd stayed home a little longer and watched the sunrise over Crystal Lake.

Distracted by her thoughts, Ember didn't notice that something wasn't right until she started to open the door and Daenerys growled low in her throat. Startled by the sound, Ember drew back, her head snapping to attention.

Deep in the building, toward the end of the hallway that divided the back half of the space, a dim light bobbed. Confused, it took her a moment to process the information: someone was inside. But that was all the time Daenerys needed. She managed to get her head inside the door before Ember let go. As Ember fumbled for her cell phone, the dog tore through the front office, emitting what could only be described as a primal cacophony of barking.

"Daenerys, no!" Ember cried. Pulling at the door, she chased after her dog without thinking.

Regardless of the fact that it sounded like the dog might kill whoever she caught, she couldn't help but be concerned for her safety. What if the intruder was armed? That thought gave her pause, and Ember stumbled briefly in the dark. As she reached for the hall light, there was a scraping noise at the other end of the hallway, and it was briefly illuminated by someone opening the outside door that led to the alley.

Although it was still dark out, there was a motion light mounted over the exit. A clear silhouette of someone larger than herself was outlined before the door slammed shut again, and she heard Daenerys thud into it.

She snapped the light on at the same instant, and relief washed through her when she saw that the dog appeared unharmed. Daenerys immediately began growling and clawing at the door. Running to it, she hoped to get a peek outside and maybe catch a better look at whoever it was, but as she passed the back-storage room, a smell stopped her.

Smoke!

Sliding to a stop, Ember fell backwards and landed hard on her bottom. The storage room was on fire.

Clambering over to her stomach and pushing up to her knees, Ember took a ragged breath and tried to control her adrenaline.

Think!

Daenerys abandoned the door when Ember fell and was quickly at her side, licking her face. Gone was the savage killer, replaced by the loyal and concerned friend.

Phone still in hand, Ember tapped out 911 as she got to her feet. "Where's the fire extinguisher?" she said aloud while waiting for the call to go through. She knew she'd seen two of them mounted in the facility, but she couldn't think clearly. Peering into the storage room, she could see a small glow of light in the middle of it, and the space was quickly filling with smoke and trailing out into the hall.

The breakroom.

"Haven 911, what's your emergency?" the dispatcher asked pleasantly.

"A fire," Ember declared, running for the breakroom. "Someone broke into the Sanctuary Animal Clinic and … there's a fire. I think he started a fire."

"What's the address?"

Clawing at the wall in the breakroom, Ember panicked for a moment when she couldn't find the light switch. When it finally clicked on, she squinted and looked frantically around. *There!* Mounted in a far corner was a small standard fire extinguisher.

"Address? Oh, the address! Oh my gosh. Can't you see it?" In her flustered state, Ember forgot that she was calling on a cell phone, which wouldn't show the dispatcher the address she was at.

Yanking the extinguisher off its hook, she then ran back out into the hall, which was now filling with smoke. Coughing once, she pulled the pin from the top of the dispenser.

"Ma'am, I need the physical address of the clinic."

Ember coughed once and tried to remember the street number. "22 … 225 Mountainview Road," she finally managed to say.

Aiming at the base of the small flames, she squeezed the trigger and swept it back and forth, spraying a broad swath of white foam.

"Ma'am, are you *inside* the building?" the dispatcher asked in alarm. "Please exit the building. Both the police and fire department have already been dispatched. Do you need an ambulance?"

"No!" Ember said quickly. Coughing again, she stepped back out of the room and tried to assess whether the fire was out. The smoke was too thick. She had to clear the air. Stepping to the back door, she didn't care anymore if the prowler was still out there. She pushed it open and kicked at the doorstop so it would stay on its own.

White smoke billowed out around her, and fortunately, the hallway cleared rather quickly. Telling Daenerys to stay, Ember crept back in and looked tentatively into the back room. She didn't see any flames. Turning the light on, she gasped at what it revealed.

The papers that had fallen to the floor while she sat there two nights ago were now piled together in the middle of the room.

Someone had set them on fire.

EIGHTEEN

Deputy Trenton tipped his hat before leaving, a half-hearted gesture that matched the crooked grin on his face.

"I don't think he's buying my theory," Ember stated, watching the door close.

Mel glanced sideways at her, a look of concern on her face. "Which one? Because I have to admit I'm having a hard time keeping track."

The scorn hurt more, coming from Mel. But Ember couldn't really blame her. What was supposed to be the ideal situation and job for her was turning into something more of a nightmare. If the clinic failed, Mel didn't have many other job options in Sanctuary, and it would probably mean she would have to move back home with her parents.

It was still barely six. The sirens had awoken Mel, as she lived right across the street, and she'd come running. It was a huge relief for Ember to see her, and she'd taken Daenerys back to her basement apartment, where she was still sleeping while they dealt with the aftermath.

The fire turned out to be nothing more than the pile of papers smoldering, and the smoke ended up being the worse of the damage. Thankfully, the floor was tile, so nothing else burned. Most of the lingering smell was isolated to the storage room, where they had the window open and a fan running. They'd been lucky.

"You're really buying into Deputy Trenton's explanation of teenagers breaking in, looking for drugs?" While Ember doubted Sheriff Walker would have thought otherwise, she still wished he was on duty.

Mel turned abruptly and went to the cold coffee pot on the back counter of the reception area. She carefully measured out the coffee grounds before disappearing into the utility room and then came back after a minute with the water. It wasn't until she'd flipped the brew switch that she faced Ember.

"Someone *did* try to hammer open the meds cabinet," she said without her normal flippant attitude. "And starting a fire like that is totally something a stupid punk would do. Why are you so convinced that it has something to do with Tom and Butterscotch?"

"Ember," Mel continued when she didn't answer right away, "I'm sorry I'm cranky, but I am *not* a morning person. I should have had about two cups of coffee by now. One extra for the stress."

Ember laughed at that and fought to prevent a tear from escaping. She didn't trust herself to talk. The reality of the scene she just experienced was threatening to overwhelm her.

"You've been through a lot this past month," Mel said with more compassion. Recognizing the internal battle, she was quick to step forward and wrap her small arms around Ember.

She hadn't been lying … she was s*trong*. Struggling to take a deep breath, Ember hugged her back, and when Mel turned it into a rocking motion that then progressed into a fumbling, twirling dance, she began to laugh out loud.

"Okay!" Ember gasped, finally breaking away from her giggling friend. "I promise, I'm not about to have a breakdown."

"Good," Mel countered, "because I don't handle them well. I never know when to be serious or joke, and I usually end up doing the wrong thing. Now," she ordered, pouring out two steaming cups of fresh coffee. "Talk."

"Those papers," Ember replied. "They're the same ones that fell over Sunday night when I was looking through the file for Black Shadow."

"Yeah, I know. I *told* you yesterday we should have picked them up!"

"Mel," Ember persisted, trying to get her to focus. Wasn't it obvious to her? "What if someone who didn't want that information shared came here this morning to *take* the evidence? But when they discovered that impossible mess, they decided to just burn it all and make it look like some random drug-seeking thief was here, rather than try and cart it all away?"

Mel silently mulled it over, sipping slowly at the coffee. "But it was blacked out."

"Maybe they don't know that. Or, they thought it would still be enough to prompt an investigation by the insurance company, were they to get ahold of it."

"Did they burn it?"

Pausing for a moment, Ember fought against her initial instinct to lie and say yes. But she needed to trust Mel. She *did* trust Mel. Shaking her head, Ember ran out to her truck and retrieved her leather bag. Bringing it back inside, she looked to make sure the front shades were drawn, but then felt silly. Maybe she *was* getting paranoid.

"I kept them with me," she explained, pulling out the folder. "But I don't know what good it'll do. Sheriff Walker seems more concerned about protecting Ellsworth's name than getting to the truth of it."

"I think you should just put that right back in your bag and wait for the autopsy results before deciding what to do with it. If anything. I still feel that what's done is done, as far as Black Shadow goes, and I don't want any part of making things worse for Doctor Bernie."

"I understand that, Mel." Ember appreciated her honesty. "And I actually agree with you. I thought a lot about it last night. If it weren't for what I'm sure was an attempt by someone to get this," she added, shaking the file in the air, "I was prepared to let it all go. Now, we'll have to wait and see."

The sun finally broke over the ridge, casting long ribbons of smoky sunlight through the room when Ember pulled the shades up. Looking around the reception area, she made a mental check of what still needed to be done. Hopefully airing it out and wiping everything down would take care of the wet campfire smell.

There was a shipment of products slated for delivery the next day, a large order of animal crates for the boarding room to be picked up in Parker, and the two exam rooms still needed to be organized and stocked. Otherwise, aside from the additional cleanup in the storage room, they were practically ready for opening day the following Monday.

Ember estimated that if they got the crates that afternoon, they could save Friday for nothing but cleaning, giving them the weekend to enjoy the parade and rodeo.

"How's the logo coming?" she asked, deciding to change the subject. She wasn't going to let things spiral out of control and ruin everything she was working so hard for.

"I thought you'd never ask!" Mel exclaimed, her whole demeanor changing. "Wait here!"

A few minutes later, she was back with Daenerys and a sketch pad. Flipping it open, she revealed her design to Ember.

"Mel! This is amazing!" and she meant it. The creative use of the letters S, A, and C in combination with the animal profiles was simply perfect.

"You really like it? Because I talked with the printing shop, and they'll convert it to a digital image with a one-time setup fee. We can have T-shirts and a banner made by Friday."

"Do it," Ember replied without hesitating. "This is just what we need to make the clear distinction between Dr. Chambers's practice and mine. And last night I checked out the profile you set up online. I like what you've done with that too. I'll dig my camera out and start posting some pictures to it, showing the remodel and local stuff."

"Even with the few cancellations after all the business with Tom and Bonnie, we still have a pretty good schedule going for the first month," Mel offered. "The doc was sure to let his old clients know you were opening, Ember. He's a good man."

"I know he is," Ember assured her. "Aunt Becky speaks very highly of him, and it takes a lot to get her respect."

Smiling more broadly now, Mel filled her cup back up. "Where do we start?"

"Why don't you go back home for the rest of the morning and get some sleep? I'll get the storage room cleaned up. If you drop me off at Becky's after lunch, I can spend some time with Butterscotch while you take my truck into Parker to get the crates."

"Uh-uh," Mel said stubbornly. "You honestly think I'm going to leave you here to this?" she demanded. "Go get the buckets, girl. We can knock this out twice as fast and go *out* for lunch before I drop you off."

A sense of calm replaced Ember's anxiety as she realized that she wasn't alone. Mel was a true friend, and while she might not believe Ember about the fire, she was still supporting her. Feeling lighter as she went to gather the cleaning supplies, she still checked to make sure the deadbolt was secured on the backdoor.

Her hand was still on the lock when a tendril of coldness slithered around her midsection. Deputy Trenton assumed, when he found no obvious sign of forced entry, that the backdoor had been left unlocked. But as she stood there, reliving the moment, Ember could clearly recall hearing the deadbolt slide open before the intruder was revealed in the light. The front doors and windows were all locked.

How did the prowler get inside?

NINETEEN

Standing with her head leaning against Butterscotch's neck, Ember could almost forget everything that was happening. They were alone in the back pasture at Becky's house, surrounded by the still woods.

It was a drastic contrast to the chaos she'd left behind in the house. Mel and Daenerys had gone inside with her so Becky's kids could get a chance to be reunited. You would have thought it was a year since they'd seen the dog rather than four days. After witnessing Daenerys being buried under several dogs and just as many kids, all fighting for her attention, Ember understood why Becky felt she'd be happier with her. It really *was* possible to be smothered by too much affection.

Gravel crunched in the distance, and Ember looked up to see Mel headed down the long driveway. Waving, she felt a small pang of sadness at the sight of Daenerys looking at her through the back window. They'd be gone a couple of hours at most. Shaking her head, Ember laughed at herself, realizing how much of an impact the dog had made on her life already. It was a good thing.

"And you," she said to the horse, giving his muscular neck a pat. "You are the picture of perfect health, my friend."

Butterscotch whinnied in response and tossed his head once. Sidestepping, he then trotted over to a nearby hitching post and rubbed his face against it.

Crossing her arms over her chest, Ember silently stared at him as he continued to prance around. How long had it been since anyone had ridden him? Becky made it sound like he was well cared for up until he was surrendered. Horses were very social animals, and being isolated and inactive for so long wasn't healthy, either physically or emotionally.

Making up her mind, Ember strode over to the barn and entered the tack room. Grabbing the necessary equipment, she then hefted a saddle over her right arm. When she reappeared and Butterscotch saw the items, he became even more excited. As she suspected, he wanted to go riding.

It was a good thing he was so mellow and well-trained, because it had been years since Ember saddled a horse. Twenty minutes later, she gave everything a final check. Last thing she wanted was to fall off.

As she swung up onto Butterscotch's back, a small thrill chased out the last of her anxiety, and she could finally take a deep breath. The world looked a little better from that angle.

Fortunately, Becky's fields were both large and well-cleared, because Ember spent over an hour galloping and trotting the large handsome horse around in them. He responded well to all of her commands, often anticipating them based on her positioning in the saddle. They were a good match.

When Ember heard a car headed their way, she thought at first that it must be Mel returning but was surprised to look up and see the sheriff's SUV. By the time Becky and Walker made their way out to her, she'd already gotten the tack back in the barn and was brushing Butterscotch down.

"I hope you don't mind that I used your gear," Ember said to Becky after nodding a hello to the sheriff.

"Of course not, Ember! I saw you galloping. I forgot how well you can handle a horse."

"It's been a long time," Ember replied. "I'm extremely rusty. What's up, Sheriff? I'm sure you heard about the fire."

Frowning, Sheriff Walker stuck his hands into the pockets of his jeans. "Trenton filled me in. Good thing you happened to be there so early, Ember. Sorry that happened to you. While I still stand by my statement that Sanctuary doesn't experience violent crimes very often, we're unfortunately still prone to the same petty thievery every city attracts. Especially during our high tourist months."

Ember's eyes narrowed slightly in response, and she pursed her lips. So, he was standing behind the drug-seeking, misguided-teen theory. "Deputy Trenton figured we must have left the back door unlocked, but I remembered later this morning that I heard the deadbolt being opened. How do you think he got in, then, Sheriff? I had to unlock the front door when I got there, and we confirmed all the windows were latched.

Sheriff Walker stared at Ember long enough that it began to get uncomfortable. Shifting her weight, she glanced at Becky and then back at the older man. "I interrupted something," she pressed, "and so I don't think he had time to finish creating the scene. I'll bet he planned on damaging the back door or a window before he left."

"Right."

Another long moment of silence increased the awkwardness until Becky had enough. "Oh, come on, Ben," she lamented. "Ember has a point. The whole situation is freaking *weird*."

Turning his hard gaze on his old friend, Walker let out a long breath. "Becky, while I can appreciate the coincidence, weird doesn't qualify as a reason to launch an investigation into the serious allegations Ember has made. Besides, that's not why I'm here. As far as I'm concerned, the break-in is cut-and-dry. We'll increase our patrols of the area and keep an eye out for any punks prowling late at night, but there isn't anything more to be done."

"Then why did you come out here?" Ember's voice held more bitterness than she intended, and the sheriff looked at her sharply.

"Ember, I don't want you to think that I've dismissed all of your concerns. But you need to understand my position here." His tone softened, and he sounded genuine. "I'm an elected official, and I'm paid by the taxpayers to investigate *criminal* activity. Even if your suspicions of Ellsworth and his horse are accurate, it's not a local law enforcement issue. If you're set on pursuing it, I assume you'd need to contact the proper state agency that investigates insurance fraud and whatever licensing board governs veterinarians, for Doc Bernie's alleged involvement. Honestly, on a personal level, I don't see what good any of that would do, but it's up to you." Taking a breath, he scratched at his jaw and seemed relieved to finally be coming to the point of his visit.

"Now, the leap that some sort of cover-up of this scam somehow led to the murder of Tom is another issue altogether, and one that I'm also happy to put to rest." The sheriff rushed to explain, before Ember could interrupt. "I got the results of the autopsy, and it was determined to be inconclusive."

"Inconclusive?" Ember echoed. "How is that possible?"

"You of all people should know that medicine often isn't an exact science," he replied. "I spoke personally with the State Medical Examiner. He explained that there were several wounds that could have been the COD, or cause of death. Two separate blows to the head resulted in massive trauma, one blunt injury to the chest cracked three ribs, forcing two of them to penetrate his lungs, though there was no pulmonary edema, or lung collapse, indicating he was already dead at the time of that injury. The puncture wound on his back pierced his descending aorta, or the large artery from the heart. Based on blood pooling, it appears that he was still alive at the time, so the ME figures it was either that or one of the head wounds that ultimately killed him."

"How can that be inconclusive?" Ember demanded, a headache beginning to throb behind her left eye.

"Because of the size of the wound. It was small, Ember, and potentially matched one of the farrier tools found by the state police when they dug through the hay for evidence. Also, the circumstances at the scene. Tom was a farrier. He was in the stall of a client's horse that he was scheduled to work on that week. Based on the evidence, as well as your professional eyewitness account, the most likely scenario is that Butterscotch caught him off guard and he fell on the hoof knife. Whether it was before or after he caught a hoof to his head is inconsequential. It would still be ruled accidental."

"Someone injected that horse with morphine!" Ember countered, her temper rising. "And it had to be someone who knew how to administer it intravenously. Like a stable owner!"

If it were possible for Walker to blush, Ember had no doubt that his face would've turned red. Nostrils flaring, the sheriff's demeanor lost any of the previous empathy. "Or a farrier! This might surprise you, but I take my job seriously. I already went out and questioned Bonnie and Carl about the morphine, Ember. It's something they keep with their supplies, mostly for issues that come up with the cattle, but it turns out Tom sometimes used it when shoeing the horses. Something that isn't that uncommon, I'm told."

Ember's head reeled. Was it possible? Looking back at the sheriff and then Becky, she tried to think it through. Butterscotch was an unknown horse. It *was* possible that Tom might have thought to give him a sedative before working on him.

"Maybe it was late," she reasoned, "and so Tom just decided to use what he found on hand. If he wasn't familiar with the difference in dosing between a regular injection and intravenous, it's possible that's how he overdosed him."

"That's plausible," Becky agreed. "I don't like to speak ill of the dead, but he wasn't the brightest crayon in the box. Except, where did the syringe go?"

"That's a good question," Walker replied. "I don't know if forensics collected the trash from the garbage cans in the barn. I'll check on it, but it may not matter." He turned back to Ember. "Since the state ruling was inconclusive, they went back to the regular exam findings, as well as the witness statements," Walker explained, his voice neutral again. "Based on those findings, both the ME—Dr. Austin—and myself agreed to declare it as an accidental death. It's over, Ember."

Nodding in understanding, Ember gave the sheriff a small smile. When he turned to walk away, the grin quickly faded. While she was more than eager to drink the Kool-Aid, her gut told her that the truth wasn't nearly that simple.

TWENTY

Ember struggled under the weight of the last box, wishing she had thought to ask the delivery guy to put them in the different rooms they belonged to. She didn't want to call for help and interrupt Mel's work in the section of the clinic that was set up as a boarding area.

They certainly weren't going to advertise boarding services, since they didn't have the manpower for it, but they were still required to have it for any animals recovering from surgery, or strays. The cages Doctor Chambers used were both small and archaic. Ember had a more modern philosophy when it came to pet care. She donated the smaller pens to Becky's shelter and replaced them with ones that were three times as big, complete with built-in food and water holders, IV access, and even heaters. One corner of the room was now a cat enclosure, complete with climbing towers and multiple litter boxes.

Dropping the box on the exam table, Ember looked around at the room. She was proud of what they'd accomplished. A fresh coat of paint and new cabinets did wonders. Not to mention updated decorations.

Catching her reflection in a small mirror over the sink, she smiled. She was wearing a brand-new clinic T-shirt with the logo Mel designed. She might not have chosen purple for the color since it clashed with her hair, but it still looked good. Apparently, Mel knew the shop owner, and he offered a two-day turnaround if they took the uniquely colored shirts.

Tearing open the package and removing the various contents, Ember's mind began to wander back to the conversation with Sheriff Walker the night before. She was trying hard to get beyond it, to simply accept the decision and "move on," as everyone else seemed so keen on doing. Maybe it had something to do with the fact that she found Tom's body, or felt responsible for Butterscotch, but images from that dreadful scene kept running through her mind. She couldn't shake it off.

She jumped when the front bell chimed, indicating that the door was opened. Daenerys sprang from where she'd been sitting close by, and Ember rushed to follow her, calling out as she went.

"Hello?"

"Ember!" Mayor Gomez exclaimed happily when she saw her. "I'm so glad you're here." Waving a couple of sheets of paper at her, she hustled toward her. "I wanted to drop off the itinerary for the parade. I've also got the parade order sheet. You'll see that you're fourth in line! It will start in the arena at the rodeo, as is customary, and stop at the playfields at the high school. You *must* be there by seven Saturday morning. It will start at eight sharp, and we simply can't be late. You have your sash, right?"

Ember nodded and then smiled at the woman's enthusiasm. It was hard not to be caught up in it just a little bit. Perhaps the weekend would turn out to be a fun time. Maybe she and Sean could watch the rodeo exhibition event Saturday night before the fireworks display. She'd mention it the next time she saw him.

Or you could call the cell number on that card Nathan gave you. The thought was random, and Ember knew she was silly for feeling guilty about it. She'd accepted one dinner date and was by no means dating Sean. However, she'd always lived by a personal rule of not even casually seeing more than one man at a time. She'd had a front-row seat to more than one bad scene due to friends that had done it.

"I've got my old mare, Bunny, available." Mayor Gomez interrupted Ember's internal conflict. "She's been in her fair share of parades, I'll tell you! I can have her there and waiting for you."

Ember hesitated. It wasn't until that moment that she knew what horse she was going to ride.

"Thank you, Mayor Gomez, but I'm going to ride Butterscotch."

"Butterscotch!" the older woman blurted, her expression changing. "Ember, I was incredibly relieved this morning when I found out Tom's death was ruled accidental. But I don't understand why you would want to flaunt that horse around. It's a parade. A celebration. No one wants to be reminded about a tragedy, and how do we know he's safe? No," she continued, shaking her head and getting more worked up. "I don't think I could allow that."

"Mayor Gomez, I don't know what you heard, but there is absolutely nothing wrong with the horse," Ember replied calmly. "He isn't sick. He was acting out because of a drug he'd been given. The most likely conclusion is that Tom administered the wrong dose. Please don't penalize Butterscotch because of that."

"Oh," the mayor muttered, clearly thinking it over. "All I heard was that it was accidental, so I made an assumption." Twirling a ring on her finger in what must be a nervous habit, she huffed once and seemingly made up her mind. "Are you certain he's parade quality, Ember? You know how stressful that can be on a horse."

Relieved that her old teacher was being reasonable, Ember relaxed. Taking one of her hands, she gave it a reassuring squeeze. "I rode him for hours yesterday, Mayor Gomez. I may be rusty, but I still know horses, and he's one of the most solid mounts I've ever been on. I'll check with his previous owner first, to get her opinion, and I'll let you know for sure by tomorrow. But I promise you, if he shows any signs of agitation, I'll immediately remove him from the lineup." Ember had a feeling that the best way to prove to everyone that both she and the horse were trustworthy was to literally parade *both* of them in front of the whole town.

"Okay, I'll trust you on this one." Glancing at her watch, the mayor turned to go. "And Ember," she continued, pausing with a hand on the front door. "It's nice to have you back in Sanctuary."

Encouraged by the kind words, Ember tackled the next stack of boxes, revealing cans of special diet dog food. *Of course,* she thought as she hefted the top box onto a nearby counter. *It would have to be something heavy.*

She was just stepping back to admire her dog food can pyramid in the waiting room corner, when her cell phone rang. She felt a small twinge of irritation when she saw the caller ID. It was Morton Ellsworth.

"Sanctuary Animal Clinic," she answered in as professional of a voice as possible.

"Dr. Burns, I'm glad I reached you. This is Morton Ellsworth. I've been meaning to call and arrange a time to meet. I just so happen to have this afternoon free, if you would be able to come by and discuss a possible schedule for routine care of my herds. I've been having Dr. Clemens in Parker handle it since Bernie left, but I'd rather keep things local."

Ember wasn't sure what to make of the offer. The sheriff made it clear the two were friends, and she didn't know how much he'd shared with the stable owner about her allegations. She figured he'd be shunning her at this point rather than offering to hire her. Intrigued, she wanted to hear what he had to say. "Sure, Mr. Ellsworth. I'd be happy to talk with you about it."

"Great!" he exclaimed. "Then I'll see you at three!"

***

Knowing Ember was a fan of coffee, he already had a pot set out in his study when she arrived. She noticed he opted for a glass of whatever liquor was in the decanter next to it.

Rather than sitting behind his desk, he chose one of the two high-backed leather chairs and then gestured for her to take the other, the same one she sat in just four days earlier.

Morton Ellsworth was much more controlled and put together than he had been the other night. Dressed in a sharp-looking blazer with a clean shave and styled hair, he was a rather handsome man. Far from the haggard and weary owner in the stables. It drove home to Ember how desperate he'd been and how close to the edge their finances must be. While

Sandy was quite drunk when she made her declarations, she probably wasn't exaggerating.

"Look, Ember," he began, clasping his hands together while leaning toward her. "I'm not going to waste your time. Shall we address the elephant in the room and get it out of the way?"

Bracing herself for what she was sure was going to be an uncomfortable confrontation, she appreciated his directness.

"Doctor Bernie Chambers is a good friend of mine. His son and I were best friends until he moved out of Sanctuary some years ago, but Bernie remained a sort of father figure to me. What happened with my stallion was preventable, but I can't and don't place all the blame on Bernie. I knew he was having some medical issues, and I should have been paying more attention. Even after what happened, I continued to use Dr. Chambers until he retired, and we all miss him very much."

Trying not to be obvious, Ember let out a long breath of relief. Confused at where the conversation was going, she reasoned the sheriff must not have said anything to Ellsworth. Or else he was simply *pretending* not to know. He was a smart man, and he knew what to say to get what he wanted.

"So, can we acknowledge that, yes, there was an unfortunate mishap last year, but that it has no bearing on our working relationship? Because I really do need a local, reliable vet."

Waiting a moment to make sure he was done, Ember then smiled at him. "What happened between you and Dr. Chambers isn't any of my concern," she said pleasantly. "Unless," she added casually, "it pertains to any of my *current* clients."

Morton's calm exterior shell waivered as a flicker of irritation darted across his features. But then he leaned back and crossed a leg over his knee. "I don't see how it would."

Ember allowed the silence to draw out just long enough to accentuate the tension, then her smile widened. "Then tell me about your cattle, Mr. Ellsworth, and what kind of care they need."

Half an hour later, after discussing past, present, and future expected needs, the stable owner left to go retrieve previous records from the office out in the barns.

Right on cue, Sandy followed in his wake, blowing into the room with such purpose that she didn't even notice Ember at first.

"Oh!" she exclaimed, after reaching the desk and opening a drawer before looking up. "You again." Dropping the folder, she splayed her hands on the desktop, leaning over it like a judge delivering a verdict in court. "This is getting to be a habit."

Determined not to be intimidated, Ember sat up straighter. "Your father invited me out to talk about working for him. As a vet," she added somewhat lamely.

Chortling, Sandy looked down her nose at her. "Sure. Whatever you want to believe."

Ember decided she liked the woman much better when she was drunk. It was amazing how, after all of these years, all the old feelings from high school came rushing back so easily. Instantly, Ember was the same young girl that was constantly teased for her looks and name. Refusing to give in to the emotions, she pushed back.

"Based on what you told me the other night, although you might not remember it so well, you might benefit from the money you'll save by hiring me over that high-priced racket out of Parker."

Raising her eyebrows, Sandy straightened and crossed her arms. Tilting her head, she appeared to be measuring an opponent before a boxing match. "How *is* the practice going? I saw your new page on Facebook. Cute."

"It doesn't officially open until Monday," Ember stated, her voice dry. "But thanks for asking."

"You're wrong, ya know."

"What?" Ember asked, watching Sandy closely.

"I remember everything I said the other night, and it was all true. I can't afford to pay for another one of father's pets."

Her face burning, Ember blurted out a retort before she could stop herself. "He seems to have a way of finding the money when he needs it, like convenient insurance policies."

Gasping, Sandy looked like she'd been slapped. "What in the hell are you talking about?"

Committed now, Ember was already kicking herself for not having more control over her mouth. It always got her into trouble. "You're the accountant. Do the math yourself, but some things are worth more dead than alive." On the verge of saying more, Ember literally bit her tongue. The exchange was so far nothing more than two women being petty. Anything further could have the potential of ruining her career in Sanctuary. She wasn't going to be that careless.

"If you're referring to Black Shadow, father donated half of that money to a local organization, against my advice," Sandy countered. "And *then* he refused to press charges against that old codger." But Ember could tell she'd gotten the other woman thinking.

The revelation of Ellsworth giving up half of the policy payout also had Ember thinking. It didn't make sense, given that according to his daughter, he was supposedly on the brink of financial ruin.

"Sandy," Ember asked, trying to sound reasonable. "Who did he donate the money to?"

Sandy stared silently at her for a moment before paling slightly. Her façade of confidence gave way to what could best be described as a flash of fear. If she was about to give an answer, Ember wouldn't find out, because Morton Ellsworth returned, a box of records under one arm.

Glancing at them both for a moment, he warmly greeted his daughter and then proceeded to go through the documents with Ember. Sandy didn't say a word about Ember's outburst to her father and actually stayed in the study for the remainder of their meeting.

As she was leaving an hour later, Ember reflected back on the encounter. For some reason, the suggestion that whoever received the insurance may have been up to something with her father hit a chord with Sandy. However, she'd already promised herself that she was going to do her best to let that all go. While it was troubling how eager everyone else in Sanctuary was to dismiss Tom's death, there was nothing to gain by pursuing unsubstantiated allegations. It would be much *easier* to fall in line with the rest of them and just do her job.

But was Sandy right? Was her father trying to buy her silence, the same way he might have bought Tom's? The thought that Ellsworth was trying to manipulate her made her skin crawl. Grinding her teeth together, Ember glanced down at the box of documents he'd sent home with her. Vowing not to forget Tom and the killer she knew was still loose in Sanctuary, she glanced at herself in the review mirror.

"I'm nobody's pet."

TWENTY ONE

Giving the last strap a tug, Ember stood back from Daenerys to evaluate the fit. The labradoodle sat obediently on the porch, her head held proudly as if to say she approved of the backpack. Happy with what she saw, Ember took out her phone and snapped a picture. Not liking the background, she called to Daenerys and repositioned her so that Crystal Lake was the backdrop instead of the house.

Hitting the share function, she typed out what she hoped would be an engaging post for the few followers the clinic page had:

I'm heading up to Parker Creek Trail right now for an afternoon hike, and this time Daenerys will be carrying her own gear. Did you know that working dogs enjoy being given such a task? In fact, most any dog that likes to accompany you on a hike is likely capable of carrying their own food and *water. I grabbed this cute dog backpack online for under $25. I'll be testing out a couple of brands, and soon the Sanctuary Animal Clinic will be offering a whole line of outdoor gear for your best friend!*

Hitting the post button, Ember was happy with the spontaneous idea that was formed as she wrote it. In the summer, Sanctuary was a hub of activity for all the campers in the surrounding national and state parks. She could easily see one end of the large reception area of the clinic being turned into a pet supply store. It would be the only one like it in town.

Feeling like her creative genius might have made up for leaving the clinic early, Ember's step was lighter as she jogged for the truck. After yesterday's meeting with Ellsworth and the exchange with Sandy, the mindless work she and Mel did for most the day was a relief. But she found herself needing something more, and with cleaning the only thing left to do before the weekend, she sent Mel home early. They still had tomorrow, Friday, to get that done. She invited Mel to go on the hike with her, but apparently, while they shared several hobbies and interests, trekking through the woods wasn't one of them.

The farther into the mountains they drove, the more relaxed Ember felt. She rolled down her window and pulled the scrunchie out of her hair, letting the wind blow it around. By the time they pulled into the trailhead parking lot, it was around three, and there were only two other cars there.

Just the way I like it.

Ember felt rejuvenated when she hopped out and called Daenerys to her. "Sit," she directed, backing up a few steps so she could take another picture. "Your fans want to know what you're doing, and we won't be able to share anything once we get started." While there was a decent signal partway in, the rest of the trail was spotty at best.

After two hours of vigorous hiking, they'd already passed the other groups of hikers on their way back out. Stopping for a break, Ember sat on an old log covered with thick, spongy moss. A huge mushroom sprang from the surface, and she laughed when Daenerys sniffed at it and then darted away.

"I wouldn't recommend them," she cautioned. "I don't trust my knowledge of fungus to risk it. But these," she added, plucking a ripe raspberry off a nearby bush, "are fabulous. Just ask the bears!"

Daenerys sniffed at the offered berry before happily devouring it, and Ember tossed a few in her own mouth. They were perfect, almost to the point of falling off the vine. Picking the last few, she then gathered her stuff together.

"Time to head back," she told Daenerys after tossing one more tasty morsel to her. "It'll get dark out here early."

An hour later, the thicker area of woods started to fill with shadows, although they still had plenty of time before nightfall. Nevertheless, a stillness fell over the forest, and an ageless, damp smell arose that heralded the dark soon to come. Compelled to move faster, Ember was jogging when her cell phone suddenly began to ring, causing her to stumble and nearly fall.

Cursing under her breath, Ember stopped and checked to see who was calling. It was her Aunt Becky. Surprised to have a signal, she figured she better answer.

"What's up, Becky?" she said breathlessly.

"What in the world are you doing?" Becky countered, skipping the pleasantries. "Running a marathon?"

"Hiking up at Parker Creek Trail," Ember explained. "Not too far from the truck, but it's already getting a bit spooky out here."

"I don't like you up there by yourself," Becky countered.

"I'm not alone! I have Daenerys with me. And bear spray," she added as an afterthought.

Laughing, Becky let it go. "I talked to Kim, Butterscotch's previous owner, about your parade idea. Although I'm still skeptical about the whole thing, she thinks it's a marvelous plan. Said that he used to do some sort of exhibition riding in his earlier years."

"That's great!" Ember began walking slowly, eager to get moving but not wanting to drop the call.

Close to her side, Daenerys pricked her ears and stopped, staring back toward an especially dense area of trees.

Pausing, Ember squinted, trying to spot what had caught her dog's attention.

W*as that movement?*

Thwack!

Both Ember and Daenerys jumped at the same time, as the sound erupted from a nearby tree. Crying out and nearly dropping the phone, Ember spun around to discover a quivering arrow only a few feet away, embedded in the trunk of a cedar.

TWENTY TWO

"Ember! What happened? Ember!"

Becky's voice was calling to Ember from a distance. Her brain catching up with what happened, she blinked rapidly and brought the phone back to her face as she frantically looked around. "Someone shot an arrow at me," she whispered.

"Hey!" she called out, finally grasping the situation. "Stop! I'm a person, not a freaking bear or deer!" At the same time that she shouted the words, Ember realized she hadn't tied a colorful bandana to her backpack like she normally did.

A second arrow went whizzing by, splintering the bark a few inches besides the first one. That wasn't a hunter mistaking them for an animal.

Crying out again involuntarily, Ember grabbed at the strap on the top of Daenerys's backpack and gave her a yank. The labradoodle didn't need any more encouragement and began running ahead of Ember, up the trail. Blinded by fear, she followed recklessly, concentrating on her dog's tail, her legs feeling numb.

"Ember! Ember!"

Becky's filtered exclamations broke through her panic, and Ember realized she'd been yelling as she ran. It must have sounded horrific to her aunt. Slowing slightly, she tried to find her voice.

"I'm okay," she croaked out, glancing behind her at the same time. "Becky?" she called, when her aunt didn't answer. "Becky, are you there?" Pulling the phone away, Ember discovered the bars had disappeared. The signal was gone.

WHAAAAA …

Up ahead of them, someone was blasting an air horn. Skidding to a stop, Ember desperately tried to think clearly. Was it help? Or someone else trying to kill her? Air horns were a common hiker tool for scaring bears away. Did someone hear her shouting?

Heavy footsteps became audible, moving in her direction.

"Hello!" A man's voice. Vaguely familiar.

Ember had just decided to respond, when Nathan came barreling around the next bend, nearly colliding with her. Putting her arms out instinctively, she found herself caught up in a strong, protective embrace.

"For cryin' out loud, Ember," Nathan barked. "Why didn't you answer me? Is there a bear? Are you hurt?"

He held her out at arm's length as he spoke, checking for wounds. Ember noticed then that he had a gun in his right hand. He was also wearing a reflective vest over his uniform, something she knew rangers were required to put on when walking the trails. What was he doing out there? The question drifted to her through a haze of confused thoughts. Shaking her head to clear it, she tried to reasonably assess the situation.

"I'm sorry," she finally replied. "I panicked, I guess. Fight-or-flight syndrome and all that." Taking deep gulps of air, Ember was acutely aware of the fact that he was still holding her. "Not a bear," she rushed to explain. "An arrow. I mean, someone s*hot* an arrow at me."

"Shit," he mumbled, looking past her and surveying the woods. "You should be wearing something bright," he scolded, his eyes drifting back to scrutinize her again. "At least your dog is properly outfitted."

Ember looked down at Daenerys sitting calmly at her feet like they'd been out for a nice evening stroll. The dog's new backpack was bright orange with reflective tape across the bottom.

"It wasn't a hunter."

Finally releasing her, Nathan holstered his weapon, his expression stern. "What else would it be?"

"It's not bow hunting season for any animals found out here," Ember pressed.

"Which is why we call it poaching," Nathan explained. "Campers have all been talking about the bears spotted out on these trails this past week. It wouldn't be surprising to catch a hunter up here."

"I might agree if they'd only shot one arrow."

Nathan raised an eyebrow.

"Two," Ember said, her voice rising. "Somebody shot a *second* arrow into the tree right next to my head *after* I yelled at them to stop."

Sticking the air horn into a pocket, Nathan then took Ember by the elbow and turned her back down the trail she'd been running on. "Show me."

"*Show* you?" she repeated, her eyes wide. "I don't want to go back there, Nathan!"

"Ember," he said calmly but with authority. "If someone intentionally tried to shoot you, I want the evidence. It'll be dark soon, and I'd like to get it now. I'm sure whoever it was is long gone, especially after hearing the airhorn. A poacher … or anyone else engaging in illegal activity, is going to want to avoid a park ranger. So, come on," he urged, tugging at her arm. "I want to get out of here before dark."

Yielding to the pressure, Ember found herself walking back the way she'd just hysterically ran. Yet, she somehow felt safe. Glancing up at Nathan, her mind drifted back to her original thought. "What are you doing out here?"

"The trailhead is part of my nightly patrol," he explained. When I saw your truck parked there, I thought I'd … well, maybe check in on you and walk with you on your way out."

Was he blushing? She smiled at him and then saw a familiar bend up ahead. Her grin faded. "I'm glad you decided to … check in on me," she replied, pulling against his hand to make him stop. "That's the spot," she said, pointing at a large cedar tree. "I remember the fallen log next to it, and the rock in front of it that looks like a gargoyle."

Chuckling, Nathan titled his head toward her. "A gargoyle?"

Shrugging, Ember failed to see why her imagination mattered. Looking more closely at the tree, she drew her brows together in consternation. "Where are they?"

Forgetting her fear from just moments before, she jogged over to the spot where her terror had unfolded. Leaning in close to inspect the bark, there was patch of splintered wood and what may have been holes, but that was all.

"They're gone," Ember announced, turning to look back at Nathan. "The arrows are gone!"

***

They were still a good couple-hundred feet from the trailhead when Ember's phone erupted with missed calls and message announcements. Before she had a chance to answer any of them, Sheriff Walker came barreling down the trail toward them.

"Nathan!" he yelled when he spotted them. "You have Ember Burns with you?"

"I'm here, Sheriff," Ember answered for him. Twilight was taking over the space around them, making it hard to discern one shadow from the next. Daenerys ran ahead and bounced around Walker's feet, happy to see him.

"Well, unless you're lethally maimed, you'd best call Becky before she has a complete coronary. She called me in an uproar, convinced you were being eaten alive by a bear!"

Nathan jogged up to Walker and spoke with him in low tones while Ember did as ordered. When Becky answered on the first ring, her voice thick and near tears, she felt horrible. Not wanting to worry her aunt any more than necessary, she gave her Nathan's explanation of a poacher.

"I told you it was dangerous to be out there by yourself!" Becky lectured, but she was clearly relieved. "I'm just so glad you're okay. Do you want to come over for a late supper? The kids would love to see you again."

"Thanks, Aunt Becky," Ember choked out, fighting her own tears. She appreciated having someone in her life that cared so much. "But I have an early morning start tomorrow. Really, I'm okay. It was all a misunderstanding."

Satisfied, Becky said goodbye, and Ember was finally able to join the men's conversation. They were gathered back at their patrol cars, heads leaning toward each other. Ember's truck was the only other vehicle there.

"There were two arrows," she said without preamble.

"Okay. There were two arrows," Nathan answered. "I never said I didn't believe you."

"But you still think it was just a poacher?"

"Poaching is actually a federal offense," Nathan explained. "It comes with a very hefty fine, and possibly even jail time. Whoever did that knew they were in real trouble if caught. It doesn't surprise me that they went and collected their arrows. Might have been checking to see if they hit anything, too, but hightailed it when they heard us coming."

Looking back and forth between the two officers, Ember felt her level of frustration rapidly increasing. "Sheriff, you don't find this odd?"

Clearly uncomfortable, Sheriff Walker pushed away from his car and put his hands on his hips. "Of course I find it *odd*, Ember. Heck, I'll even go so far as to say I find it disturbing. But what I *don't* have is a motive, a suspect, or even a weapon! So, I don't know what it is you want me to say, other than you should probably wear some bright gear next time and maybe not go hiking alone."

Nathan calmly took in the exchange, squinting in thought. "I feel like I'm missing something here."

"Ember has a bit of a conspiracy theory regarding an incident with our old vet being somehow tied into Tom's death."

Ember closed her eyes. When Walker put it that way, it made her sound ridiculous. She was suddenly very tired.

"How would anyone possibly know you were out here?" the sheriff pushed. "And even if you were right, it's a huge leap to say someone tried to kill you."

He had a couple of good points. Thinking about it, something clicked into place. Ember glanced down at her phone before holding it out to Walker. "Because I posted about it before coming up here," she told him. "And I don't think they were trying to kill me, I think *she* is trying to scare me."

"She?" Nathan asked, but Sheriff Walker was already scowling.

"Sandy Ellsworth," Ember offered. "She follows our website, and I happen to know that she's an expert shot with a compound bow."

TWENTY THREE

Friday morning came way too fast, and Ember was unprepared for how much the hiking scare got to her. After a fitful sleep, she dragged her sore body out of bed but took twice as long to get ready, going through the motions like a robot. She texted Mel to let her know she was running late and to take her time getting to the clinic.

Standing at the bathroom sink, brushing her teeth, Ember felt like she was staring at a stranger. Fear had transformed her features, making her look older and harried.

I'm letting them get to me, she realized, and the thought caused a welling of hot anger to bubble to the surface. Her eyes flashed, and she spat once into the sink before stepping back. This was *her* home. *Her* town. No one was going to manipulate her or force her out of Sanctuary.

Stomping out to the kitchen, Ember grabbed the box that Ellsworth had given her and slammed it down on the table. Then, snatching her leather bag from its spot near the front door, she dug out the file for Black Shadow and set it on top of the box. Thinking for a moment, she spun around and walked with purpose to the guest room she was using as an office, Daenerys trailing behind her, and came back with a copy of her sworn witness statement for both the "accident" scene and the examination of Tom's body. Laying those sheets of paper on the table beside the box, she crossed her arms over her chest and spent a couple of minutes staring at it.

"I'm missing something," she said to Daenerys.

Shaking her head, she gathered the loose papers together and put them all in her bag. Looking at the remaining box in disgust, she then glanced down at Daenerys who was watching her earnestly.

"I'm taking that back on Monday. I might not be able to prove anything, but I'm *not* going to get caught up in whatever scam he has going or be the target for his psycho daughter."

Daenerys's ears sprang up, and she surprised Ember by leaping to her feet and barking. It wasn't until she ran for the front door that she realized there was a car coming up the driveway.

Pulling back the curtains, Ember groaned when she saw Sheriff Walker getting out of his vehicle. *What now?*

"You're making the rounds early," she stated after opening the front door.

He leaned against the railing on the front porch and reached down to scratch at the labradoodle's ears. "I wanted to catch you before you went into town," he explained. "Mel told me you were still out here. You okay?"

His concern seemed genuine, and Ember softened a little. "I'm fine. Just slept in. Would you like some coffee?"

Waving a hand, he then patted his generous stomach. "I already had my fill. Mel forced me to drink a cup of her special French press blend. It's actually pretty good."

Smiling in response, Ember wondered if they would discuss the weather next. It was obvious he had something to say, and she wasn't in the mood for indirectness. "What do you need to talk to me about?"

"I wanted you to know that even *before* Becky called and demanded I do my job or retire, I tracked down Sandy Ellsworth."

Ember could imagine the very animated conversation with her aunt and suppressed a laugh. It would have been bad timing. Walker was trying to be serious. Curious as to what he found out about Sandy, she instead tilted her head. "And?"

"Ember, Sandy was at the rodeo fairgrounds the whole afternoon and was still there when I finally found her at eight last night. Without telling her *why* I was asking, I was able to determine she took over the booth at three, for a six-hour shift. I happen to be good friends with the gentleman running a display next to her, and he confirmed she was there the whole time, without anyone relieving her. In fact, he looked after things for her while she used the restroom because she was alone."

Tapping her socked foot on the boards of the patio, Ember mulled over the information. It certainly blasted a very large hole in her theory. Unless— "So, she had someone else do it."

Straightening, Walker took his hand from Daenerys's head and pointed it at Ember. "I'd suggest you be mindful of the company you're in when you think out loud."

Blushing, Ember didn't back down. "What do you expect me to do? Someone doesn't like the information I've dug up, and they're trying to intimidate me!"

"I didn't say I disagree with you, just that you need to stop broadcasting everything. And maybe not let your personal feelings cloud your judgment when making accusations."

Stunned at the suggestion that Walker might actually believe her, she almost missed the insinuation that there was something more to her involvement. She hadn't a clue what he was referring to.

"Sheriff, you're right about me running my mouth. It's why I'm a vet and you're the law. I have no idea how to do your job, so it's a relief to know that you're looking into things. Thank you. But as to whatever personal feelings you think I have about any of it, you're missing the mark. Care to expand upon that?"

Staring back at her, Walker pursed his lips, apparently considering his reply. Shaking his head, he slapped at his leg as he pushed off from the railing. "It's none of my business, I suppose. But do me favor, will you? Let's get through this weekend, and Monday we'll sit down and go back over things. I'm responsible for the safety of the people in this county, and I take that very seriously. Now, just because I don't check in with you and detail all that I'm doing doesn't mean I'm not exploring things. I'm talking to people, Ember, and I haven't completely closed the book yet on Tom's death. Just be satisfied with that for now and let me do my job, okay?"

Ember was more than happy to relinquish any sense of obligation, now that she knew Walker wasn't letting it go. Relieved, she smiled thankfully at him. "Absolutely," she answered. "Trust me, there's nothing I'd like more than to relax and have some fun this weekend."

***

After stopping by Becky's to reassure her aunt that she wasn't dead, Ember finally made it to the clinic around ten. In spite of Ember's urging, Mel already had a big head start on her.

When she and Daenerys entered, they were greeted by a large banner spread out on the front counter. On the left end was the clinic logo, followed by the words: Dr. Burns, Local Royalty & Animal Specialist. Trying not groan, Ember knew that in spite of the corniness, it was appropriate for a parade sign.

"Ember!" Mel shouted as she ran out, a dust pan in one hand. "Your post from yesterday has over twenty shares and two hundred likes! You better start ordering the animal hiking gear you promised, because it's going to take us places."

Laughing, Ember took the dust pan from her. "Good. I'm thinking over there," she suggested, waving the pan toward the tower of canned dog food. "If I get one of those full wall display racks and a couple of turnstile ones to space out in front of it, I think we can have a decent little selection of goods."

"Yes!" Mel squealed. "I tried to get Doc Bernie to do something like that for *months*, but Marissa shot down all my ideas. And of course, Doc listened to her." Taking Ember's hand, she dragged her back to the breakroom. "Here," she urged, pouring a dark brew of coffee from her French press. "Try this. You're going to love it. Once you drink it made this way, you'll never go back to drip."

Grabbing some creamer from the small fridge she'd bought for the room, Ember noticed a new

Cylon toaster on the counter. "Where on earth did you find that!" she exclaimed. It was awesome.

"You can find anything online," Mel said. "Wait until you see the blanket that's coming!"

"Oh my gosh, this really is good," Ember praised, taking another sip of the extremely strong coffee. Reaching for more sugar, she doctored it up a bit more than usual.

"Are you going to tell me what happened last night?" Mel asked, her tone turning more serious. "Because Becky called me twice, asking if I had heard from you, and then Sheriff Walker was looking for you this morning. I mean, you answered my text last night, saying you were fine and all, but you didn't say what was going on."

Stalling, Ember took another long sip while mulling over what she should and shouldn't say to Mel. She didn't want to upset her, and Walker's words of caution weighed heavily on her. While she wanted to confide in someone, it was probably best to wait and see what the sheriff came up with next week before dragging anyone else into it.

"I was stupid and was wearing my silver backpack over a green T-shirt. I guess someone mistook me for a deer or bear or something and almost shot me."

"What!" Mel gasped. "Oh my gosh! Did they realize what they did?"

Not wanting to lie, Ember chose her words carefully. "It wasn't a gun; it was an arrow. I was so startled that I ran away. When Nathan and I went back—"

"Who?"

"Nathan Sparks, a park ranger. I met him the other day when I bought my forest pass. He saw my truck at the trailhead and went looking for me."

"Oh, really?" Mel questioned, batting her lashes. "And so, this Nathan guy came to your rescue?"

Laughing, Ember appreciated the way Mel could turn anything negative around. "Yup! No shining armor, but he is kinda cute."

Eyes widening, Mel leaning forward. "Well? What happened?"

"Oh, the arrows were gone when we got back, and it was getting dark so he wanted to get off the trail."

"Who in the world would be out shooting with a bow this time of year? That's just stupid."

"Yeah," Ember agreed, doing her best to not reveal her true feelings about it. "Nathan said the fines for poaching are really big, so whoever did it took off. Sheriff Walker met us at the trailhead because Aunt Becky convinced him I was out there dying."

"What about Nathan?" Mel pressed. "Get a number?"

"I've already got his number," Ember countered, eliciting an approving laugh from Mel. "But, Nathan *did* say he'll be in town tomorrow for the parade and stuff, so maybe you'll get a chance to meet him."

Before Mel could press her for more information, the front door chimed, and Sean called out for Ember. Looking at each other, both girls raised their eyebrows.

"Do you have to tie up every eligible bachelor in town?" Mel whispered. "Just remember that the sheriff's son is off limits. I've already called dibs."

Throwing a dishtowel at her friend, Ember went out to see Sean. They hadn't spoken for a few days, and she'd been starting to think he wasn't interested anymore. Seeing him leaning casually against the counter in his white doctor's coat, she couldn't help but think how striking he was.

"Hey, Ember," he said warmly. "Ben told me what happened with the poacher last night. Glad you're okay."

"Thanks," she said, trying not to be irritated. She knew word would get around, but she expected it to come from friends of Becky's after she talked to everyone over the weekend, not the sheriff. Although, the information was likely to be more accurate. So maybe it *was* better that way.

"Who would have ever thought that living in Sanctuary would end up being more dangerous than the big city?"

"You have a point there," Ember agreed. "Although the views here are much better."

"Maybe," Sean countered. "Look," he continued, taking a step and narrowing the space between them. "I wanted to share my good news with you. I just got word that I've been selected for the position I told you about."

"That's great!" Ember couldn't help but notice the tension growing as he moved closer. What was it about the man that made him so enticing? "When do you have to start?" Her spirits fell when she realized this meant Sean would be moving away from Sanctuary.

"Not until the fall," he replied. "Plenty of time for me to convince you that city life is better."

Blushing, Ember wasn't sure how to respond, but he was suddenly being pretty bold about his interest in her. "You'll have to work hard then," she countered. "Because I made a promise to my mom that I'd make this clinic successful, and I'm awfully stubborn once I've made up my mind to do something."

"I'm sorry to hear that," he said, moving away. "But how about dinner to help me celebrate? The Rusty Wagon Wheel is having a rib special tonight."

Enjoying the cat-and-mouse antics more than she should, Ember smiled at him. "Dinner would be nice, but I'll have to take a raincheck. I have hours of work left to do here still, and I have to be up by five in the morning to get to the parade on time. Mayor Gomez will skin me alive if I'm late."

His smile faded. "Oh. Well, I spoke with Vanessa."

The abrupt change in subject threw Ember off, and she struggled to keep up. "Yeah? What did she say?"

"That Tom had been spending his money faster than he made it and was trying to find a lender to give him a loan for the garage."

Ember pondered the information. She wasn't sure it was helpful. "Well, thanks for asking."

When Sean turned to leave without trying to persuade her to change her mind about dinner, Ember was disappointed he gave up so easily.

"Hey!" she called out.

He stopped and looked back at her. His expression was a mix of hope and concern and made him appear vulnerable. She acted impulsively and ran up to him, giving him a hug.

"Congratulations on the job, Doctor Austin. Can we celebrate with some fair food tomorrow night at the rodeo, and then maybe watch the fireworks?"

Flashing a warm smile, he hugged her back. "It's a date."

TWENTY FOUR

"Whoa, Butterscotch."

The large horse sidestepped briefly before settling down and moving to the open spot being held for them. In spite of allowing what Ember thought was plenty of time, she was still running behind schedule. Not by much, but just enough to be cutting things close and adding more anxiety to an already stressful event.

Sitting atop the quarter horse, Ember felt ridiculous. She'd spent *way* too much time on her hair and makeup. The hot pink sash stood out in painful starkness against the purple T-shirt, and she could only imagine how it all looked in contrast to her bright-red hair. The large banner was draped across the back of the horse, and what felt like a great marketing plan only the day before, now had her fearing she came across as unprofessional and a clown.

At least Butterscotch seemed to be in his element. Though spirited, he was still easy to manage and was getting along fine with the other animals in line. This caused Ember to think about Daenerys, and although she knew the dog was perfectly okay inside the clinic, she still felt bad leaving her behind.

"Oh my goodness, Ember, look at you!"

Startled out of her thoughts by the loud squeal, Ember discovered Mayor Gomez standing to her left, clapping her hands together gleefully.

"You are absolutely beautiful! And look at that banner. Mel really outdid herself with that logo. It's simply perfect! Do you have candy? No candy? Here." The older woman dug in a large satchel hanging over her shoulder and pulled out a plastic bag covered with red, white, and blue stripes. Handing it up to Ember, she then clapped her hands again, only to hop back when the sound caused Butterscotch to flinch.

Ember laughed and then quickly covered it up by thanking Mayor Gomez. "I'm sure the parade will be a hit! You've done a great job."

The mayor appeared pleased at the compliment and then moved on to the next entry in the lineup: an antique covered wagon being pulled by four huge draft horses. It was complete with a red-checkered tarp and men dressed as rough cowboys in the driver's seat.

Located farther back in the parade were several floats, the high school marching band, and logging trucks. Ember's favorite exhibition was the Native American Circle Drum group and Pow Wow Dancers. It was hypnotic to watch.

Moments later a whistle was blown, signaling the start of the procession. Sitting up as straight as possible, Ember decided to make the best of it. Waving regally with one hand, she sporadically tossed candy to the kids with the other. Butterscotch was more than able to follow the horse in front of him, which happened to be carrying the current reigning Miss Sanctuary Rodeo Queen of 2018.

The sky was broken up by scattered clouds but it was an otherwise sunny day, with the temperature expected to reach the eighties again. That early in the morning it was still a pleasant seventy. The smell of roasting peanuts, kettle corn, and fresh hay all mingled together to create the prefect atmosphere for a small-town celebration.

A huge banner was stretched across Main Street, between city hall and the post office, that read: 100 Years of Sanctuary. Ember had just passed under it and was starting to relax and enjoy herself, when a large commotion started from somewhere behind her in the line.

Twisting in the saddle, she leaned out as far as she dared, but she couldn't see what was happening. A small spotted pony darted past, dragging a little turned-over wagon behind it that used to hold bottles of water. The sides of the street were crammed with people watching the parade, and they grabbed for their kids that were darting out to collect the thrown candy.

Someone screamed.

When Ember heard the barking, she didn't recognize it at first because it was so frenzied, but when yet another horse sprinted past, its rider doing its best to get it under control, a horrible suspicion rose to the surface. Turning Butterscotch so she could see behind them, she began to hear Mel yelling.

"Daenerys! Daenerys, stop!"

Her worst fears confirmed, Ember watched the parade procession behind her part in various directions as the barking got louder. Before she had a chance to react, the nearest draft horse pinned his ears back, snorted once … and then bolted. The other horses followed suit, and as Daenerys emerged and darted behind the wagon, the draft horse was already moving for the far side of the road and the cleared crossroad beyond city hall.

Crying out in alarm, Ember managed to hang on as Butterscotch lurched forward to avoid being trampled, but not before the back end of the covered wagon clipped her right arm.

Ignoring the pain, Ember watched in horror as the wagon headed for the crowd that stood between them and the other road. The man holding the reigns was doing his best to pull at the ancient hand break, but it wasn't working.

"Daenerys! Daenerys, come here!"

At the sound of Ember's voice, the dog stopped, looking for her in the throng of people.

From beyond the front of the parade line-up, another horse came galloping up the road toward the melee, and Ember was shocked to see Nathan astride it. Weaving effortlessly through the row of parade entries, he brought his stallion alongside the charging draft horses. Grabbing the lead horses bridle, he yanked against it, calling out for it to stop. The action caused the panicked horses to slow down and allowed the spectators enough time to get out of the way. Together, he and the wagon driver brought the team to a stop, and a cheer rose up from the crowd, like it had been a grand show that was planned all along.

At the same time, Daenerys spotted Ember and ran in her direction. A new flood of panic washed over her as she realized that Butterscotch was likely to be the next target of her dog's bizarre behavior. Fumbling with the stirrups in her rush to dismount, Ember was still on the horse's back when Daenerys reached them. Freezing, she held on as Butterscotch calmly turned to face the dog only a few feet away now.

To her complete amazement, instead of barking and nipping, Daenerys sat calmly in front of the large horse. Snorting, Butterscotch took a step forward, bent his big head down, and allowed the labradoodle to lick his nose.

TWENTY FIVE

"Ember, I'm so sorry! I don't know how she got out. I swear, I locked the doors!" Mel was the first to reach them and took Butterscotch's reigns when Ember handed them to her.

Her friend was in tears, and Ember put a comforting arm around her shoulders. She had no doubt that Mel was telling the truth.

Everyone was quickly recovering from the disruption and getting back in line. The band was already starting a new song. Having bent down to pick up a quivering Daenerys, Ember stood with her as Nathan rode up. Hopping down in one smooth motion, he noticed she was wincing.

"You're hurt."

It wasn't a question as much as it was an observation. "I'm fine," Ember lied, trying to ignore the throbbing pain in her right arm. "It's just a bruise. I thought you didn't ride?" she asked, nodding at the horse. "That was an impressive display."

Nonplussed, he took the dog from her. "You're bleeding. And I said I never got into riding, not that I wasn't good at it."

Thankful for both the help and distraction, Ember examined her arm and saw that he was right. Her shirtsleeve was torn, and a wide swath of blood was spreading out from it.

Worried more about the other parade-goers, she looked around and tried her best to ascertain the damage. To her surprise, it looked like the procession was already getting back underway. She'd been picturing scattered bodies, so it was a huge relief. The small pony was being led back past them, its wagon now upright. The woman pulling on its reigns cast an angry look her way.

Nathan used both his uniform and horse to make the crowd part for them so he could lead Ember and Mel onto a side road. He was still holding Daenerys, and she appeared to have calmed down while in his grasp. She'd been cowering, so at least this time she knew she'd done something wrong.

"Ember!"

Groaning at the sight of Mayor Gomez rushing up the sidewalk, Ember looked pleadingly at Nathan. "Lord help me."

"Ember Burns, this is simply unacceptable! That's your dog, isn't it?"

When Ember only looked at her feet, the woman continued, ignoring the inquisitive eyes of the many people standing around them. "Someone could have been seriously hurt! As it is, I've had to send a handful of people over to the clinic for scrapes from falling down. I'm sorry, but I'm going to have to ask you to leave the parade and secure your dog."

"That's what I'm attempting to do," Ember replied somberly. It didn't matter how it had happened. The blame would all land squarely on her. She suspected her dog getting out wasn't accidental. Someone knew Daenerys would cause a scene, and even more … run straight for her. If it hadn't been for the uncharacteristic behavior of both the horse and the labradoodle, she probably *would* have been seriously hurt.

This realization did nothing to lighten her mood.

"Elly Gomez, are you seriously *lecturing* Ember!"

Ember groaned even louder. Her Aunt Becky had a way of walking in on situations at just the right moment. The last thing she needed was a scene with the mayor in front of everyone. There was already enough story material involving her to fuel the town for months.

"Becky, it's okay." But Ember's attempt at intervening backfired.

"No, Ember, it's *not* okay! Look at you. Look at her!" she emphasized to Mayor Gomez. "She's hurt and probably traumatized, and instead of helping her, you're taking this opportunity to criticize her?"

The mayor was momentarily speechless, but Ember knew she'd recover quickly. It was time to make a hasty exit.

"Mel, could you please take Butterscotch back to the stables at the rodeo? The trailer I borrowed from Becky is there. If you can wait with him for me, I'd really appreciate it. I need to check the clinic and put a Band-Aid or something on this," she added, flapping her injured arm.

Nodding, Mel turned and began to lead the horse away without saying another word. Becky stepped up to Nathan and took Daenerys from him before Ember could stop her.

"I'll take Daenerys with me," her aunt stated. "The kids would love to play with her for the afternoon. You can pick her up when you drop Butterscotch off, but I want you to get that arm seen to first! Come on, Mayor," Becky commanded as she turned without waiting for an answer from Ember. "Walk with me."

The mayor hesitated for a moment, started to say something, and then thought better of it. Huffing, she turned on her heel and followed after Becky, who was already headed down the sidewalk.

Laughing at the retreating women, Nathan put a hand on Ember's good arm. "Give me a minute, and I'll walk you to your clinic. I just need to find someone to take my horse."

Although thankful for his offer, Ember had an overwhelming desire to be alone. She was afraid she'd burst into tears at any moment, and that wasn't something she wanted Nathan to see.

"Thank you, but I'll be okay," she managed to choke out. "Really. I just … I just need to process this." She started back peddling before he could try and stop her, but it was unnecessary. He respected her plea and simply stood watching her retreat.

The walk back to her building wasn't pleasant, her paranoia convincing her that everyone was staring. Halfway there, she removed the Rodeo Queen sash and tried to stuff it in her pocket, but it wouldn't fit. Balling it up, she then wished she could cover up her T-shirt and the logo. Although she knew not e*veryone* was talking about her, she did overhear parts of a few conversations.

Isn't that the vet? The one whose dog …

Yeah, that's her. You'd think a vet would know how to control …

I know I won't be taking my dog there …

Ember stopped when she heard the last comment. Turning, she was prepared to give the woman who said it a piece of her mind, but discovered two very old ladies with their heads bent toward each other. Her anger instantly evaporated.

She couldn't blame them.

The optimism she'd felt the day before was wavering. What if she really was destined to fail? Picking up her pace, Ember jogged the last half-block to the animal clinic. Breathless by the time she reached the door, she wasn't surprised to find that it was ajar. Whoever unlocked it was becoming bolder and leaving a clear message. Someone who was aware of the accusations she'd made and stood to lose something if she was right. Someone who also knew of Daenerys's behavior toward horses.

Slamming the door behind her and locking it, Ember bravely checked each room before finally stopping in one to wash the wound on her arm. There was about a two-inch gash that was quite deep, and it was getting harder to lift her arm. Digging through one of the drawers in the exam room, she came up with some gauze and taped it on as best she could. It was already stained through by the time she finished. Sighing, Ember knew it wasn't going to be enough.

A pounding erupted from the front of the clinic.

Jumping and dropping the roll of medical tape in her hand, Ember then cautiously poked her head out into the hallway. Someone was banging on the front door.

"Open up, Dr. Burns! I know you're in there!"

Carl Hathaway. What was he doing there?

"I need to talk to you, now!" The pounding got louder.

What did he want? Come to think of it, one of the horses that ran past in the parade had looked familiar. Closing her eyes, Ember made a decision. Slipping out into the hallway, she ran for the back door and slid the deadbolt open. Glancing back once, she confirmed he hadn't spotted her and then stepped out into the alley.

It was all too much. Partially blinded by the tears she couldn't hold back any longer, Ember ran the two blocks down the alley toward the health clinic. She was hoping Sean could help her with both the stitches and dealing with Carl.

She was out of breath by the time she got there and took a moment to lean against the small monument out front dedicated to the contributors of the clinic. Wiping at her face, Ember did her best to pull it together. She didn't need to give anyone more to talk about. By the time she walked into the waiting room, her tears had dried.

"Hello, Dr. Burns," the receptionist greeted her warmly, recognizing her from when she came in for Tom's exam. "I'm afraid Dr. Austin is in with a patient right now."

"That's okay. I'm here to be seen," Ember explained, pointing at the bandage on her right arm. A nasty-looking bruise was taking form, already spreading hallway down her upper arm. "Just some stitches and maybe an x-ray."

"Of course!" the young lady replied. "There are a couple of people ahead of you, but it shouldn't take too long."

Turning around to face the waiting room, Ember found two other people sitting in the plush chairs. One was an older woman who looked to have a bad cold, and she smiled back at her. But the other was a younger man with two badly scraped elbows and a dark scowl.

Instantly on guard, Ember spun back around. "Actually," she called out to the retreating medical assistant. "Would it be okay if I waited in Dr. Austin's office?"

Hesitating, the woman then shrugged her shoulders. "Sure, why not join the party? It's through those doors. Last room on the right."

Eager to retreat, Ember didn't think too much about what she said. Darting through the double doors, she welcomed the quiet solitude in the hallway beyond. It was obviously the administrative area, and it appeared that everyone else was gone for the weekend. Following the directions, she went to the end and pushed the door open marked "Clinic Director."

It was a large, impressive office, with rich wood features and an abundance of expensive-looking furniture. Her eye was drawn to the largest piece opposite the door: a massive desk with a built-in bookcase behind it. Centered in the bookcase was an 8x10 photo in a silver frame. It was of Sean, and he was with a familiar, attractive blonde woman. They were both holding compound bows.

At the same time Ember spotted the picture, the door she'd pushed open swung shut, revealing the rest of the room … and the two people seated in it.

"Hello, Ember. We didn't expect to see you here," Morton Ellsworth said smoothly, his daughter at his side.

TWENTY SIX

Spinning to face them, Ember tried to think clearly. What were they doing there? Why was Sandy in a picture with Sean?

"I don't think Ember was expecting to see us, either," Sandy offered. But gone was the cynicism from her voice. She was perched on the arm of the leather chair her father occupied. Dressed in faded jeans and a flannel shirt, she looked to be playing the part of a ranch hand today, and the role suited her. Her expression was thoughtful, but any hint of playfulness was gone.

Backing away slowly as she processed the scene, Ember bumped into the desk. Skirting around it, she felt better with the obstacle in between them, what little good it would do.

"I imagine you might have some questions," Morton continued, looking somewhat concerned. "Actually, that's also why we're here." He was interrupted by the door opening again, and Sean walked in.

He must not have been informed he had guests, because he appeared utterly shocked and looked rapidly from one person to the next. "What's this?" he barked, settling his gaze on Morton. "I told you not to ever come here!"

Shaking his head, Morton Ellsworth folded his hands in his lap. "Sean, we're beyond that now."

"I don't know what you're talking about," Sean retorted, crossing the room in four long steps. Without even acknowledging Ember, he went to a cabinet against the far wall and removed a bottle of liquor and a cup. Something she doubted the clinic board would approve of.

There was another door beside the cabinet, and Ember figured it either led to a bathroom or was another exit. Sean lingered near it, sipping at the drink he'd poured sloppily, spilling several drops onto the floor. He didn't offer any to his guests.

"I've been hearing some disturbing rumors," Ellsworth continued, pointing at Sean. "One of them I already tried to address, but it would seem our good Dr. Burns has higher morals than the lot of us. A nice paycheck isn't going to be enough this time to buy her silence."

Sean finally looked fleetingly at Ember and then back down at his drink. "I told you, I don't know what you're talking about. Now, leave my office. All of you."

Before anyone could either object or comply, the door opened yet again. This time, Sheriff Walker's large form filled the entry. Ember's first reaction was relief, but when she saw the look exchanged between him and Ellsworth, a fresh wave of fear blossomed.

Was there anyone in this town she could trust?

"What the hell!" Sean blurted, slamming the drink down on the corner of the desk and splashing some of the amber liquid. "If you all want to have a meeting, why don't you do it over at the station and leave me out of it?"

"I'm afraid we can't do that," Walker said. His tone left no room for argument.

Ember felt like she'd snuck into the back of a theatre and was witness to the closing act. She had no idea what was going on, but was afraid to say something at the risk of being kicked out. At the same time, she wanted to flee. Conflicted, she decided to give it a few more minutes to see where it was going.

"I asked the sheriff here to join us," Morton explained. "When I found out he was snooping around, asking questions about my daughter, I did some of my *own* digging. Sean, this has gone too far."

"Shut up!" Sean yelled, spittle flying from his lips. "Shut your mouth, Morton!"

"Don't speak to my father like that, Sean," Sandy cautioned. "You may have gotten away with it with me, but I won't be intimidated by you anymore."

"Wait," Ember interrupted without thinking. "Sandy is Sean's ex-wife?"

"You didn't know that?" Walker replied, confirming it for her.

"How would I have known? Nobody ever told me!"

"I guess I just assumed you knew," Walker explained. "And Sean suggested you were targeting Sandy out of jealousy."

Sandy snorted at that, making Ember feel even more foolish. "*Targeting* Sandy?" Ember repeated, turning an incredulous gaze on Sean. "Why would you say something like that? Unless …" she trailed off, lost in thought.

When Sean finally looked up to meet her stare, for the first time, she found his eyes cold and dangerous.

"Because he has a lot to lose," Morton finished for her. "And I'm afraid I've unwittingly played a role in something much more nefarious than it was ever meant to be."

"You were just trying to protect the stables," Sandy said softly, turning to her father.

"Stop trying to sound so noble," Sean countered. His voice dripped with contempt.

"It was his idea," Morton explained, pointing at Sean. It wasn't accusatory but said as a matter-of-fact. "What isn't common knowledge is that the purchase of Black Shadow wasn't a lone venture for me. I had an investor."

"Sean," Walker said, stating the obvious.

Nodding, Morton patted his daughter's leg. "My daughter tried to caution me against involving her ex-husband in the stables, but I wouldn't listen. Sean contributed a third of the needed funds. Sandy didn't know about it until I told her yesterday. A year after the purchase, we'd made less than half of our initial investment back, so we were still … partners, you could say."

Sean crossed his arms overs his chest and leaned against the cabinet, resolved to the fact that their secrets were being aired.

"Six months later," Morton continued, "when I got a second callback for Black Shadow's stud service, I suspected something might be wrong. It's not uncommon for the mare not to get pregnant the first go-around every once in a while, but not two in a row. Using a blind, outside lab, I confirmed my worst fears."

"Black Shadow *was* sterile!" Ember exclaimed.

"Yes," Morton replied. "Obviously, he was tested prior to his purchase, and those results were part of the required documents for the insurance coverage. There was nothing wrong with him for a year and a half. I cautioned Sean against pushing the stallion too hard when he demanded we expand his schedule. And I suspect Sean may have administered some drugs I didn't approve of."

When Sean didn't deny any of it, Morton simply shook his head. "At twenty thousand a service, with five outstanding fees to be refunded, that amount alone was enough to practically bankrupt me," he continued. "I was desperate. Didn't know what to do. When I went to Sean, he was just as concerned at first, but he quickly came up with a plan, one I was adamantly against at first. Until the third breeder called me up, demanding either a second service or refund. But the money was already spent." Rubbing a hand through his hair, the stable owner at least looked ashamed.

"Bernie—Doctor Chambers—had been having a rough go of it. The week before, I'd stopped him from giving the wrong medication to one of my cows, and that was what gave Sean the idea in the first place. He confided in me that he'd recently diagnosed the doctor with early dementia."

Ember gasped at that, and Sean gave her a sharp look. "So much for doctor-patient confidentiality, huh?" she asked, not expecting an answer.

"Yeah, it was wrong," Morton agreed. "But it was the key to making the whole dosage scheme believable. Black Shadow already had the festering wound, so the scenario was plausible. I didn't see any other way out."

"So, you framed a man that was supposed to be your friend?" Sheriff Walker barked, his anger clearly visible. "Made him believe that he killed your horse, and ended his career!"

Hanging his head in disgrace, Morton spoke barely above a whisper. "It would have all been okay after that, except that Sean got greedy. We'd made an agreement that we wouldn't sue Doc Bernie. The insurance would cover the outstanding stud fees and would pay out the life insurance. I'd "donate" half of it to Sean's medical center as a cover, and that would be it. But then he came to me one afternoon and said he'd changed his mind. He wanted to sue."

Looking up, Morton pointed again at Sean. "You just had to have more, didn't you? Tom overheard us arguing," he explained, turning back to the sheriff. "I didn't know he was in one of the stalls. Only way I could get him to promise not to tell anyone was to hire him on full-time at more than double what he would normally make. Sean backed off from suing, and I thought that was the end of it."

"You can't prove any of this," Sean said evenly. His face was a mask of barely-contained fury, his eyes dilated and dark.

"I still have the papers," Ember revealed.

When Sean slowly turned toward her, she tried not to flinch.

"I'm guessing that was you in my clinic the other night? Well, the papers weren't there, Sean. I still have them."

"It doesn't matter," he said through clenched teeth. "My name is nowhere on them, and aside from the word of this admitted fraud," he added, gesturing toward Morton, "there's no way to prove otherwise."

Ember couldn't believe his audacity. The man really believed he was untouchable. Then, it dawned on her. This was all about his job in the city. About getting out of Sanctuary. Her own anger growing now as she understood he was the one behind everything that was happening to her, she leaned toward him against the desk.

"You're right, Sean. It doesn't matter."

He blinked at her, not understanding.

"Your violation of the state privacy law alone is enough to get you fired from your precious dream job. In fact, just the *investigation* my complaint is going to cause will probably be enough."

The truth to her statement couldn't be denied. As Sean realized this, his whole demeanor changed, and Ember saw a hint of madness cross his features.

"You have the knowledge and access to morphine," Ember continued, her mind racing as the undeniable truth began to surface. "And Tom was already draining Ellsworth. So, tell us, how much did he get from *you*?"

"Oh my gosh, Sean, what did you do?" Sandy breathed. Standing, she took a step back, away from her ex-husband.

"You almost got away with it," Walker said, moving deeper into the room, between Sean and the Ellsworths. "You thought you had everything covered, but you didn't count on Ember being so … thorough."

"It was an accident!" Sean yelled, his façade finally breaking. "It wasn't supposed to happen! I didn't want it to happen!" Stumbling backwards, he put his hands out and slid along the wall, retreating away from them.

"You killed him!" Morton shouted, springing to his feet. His voice was thick with emotion. "Why, Sean?"

"The first time Tom came to me was in April," Sean gushed, looking pleadingly at Morton. His eyes were wide and wild. "He demanded fifty thousand dollars, or else he'd expose us and destroy my career."

Laughing hysterically, Sean appeared to be a different man. "The fool had no idea what he was doing. I didn't have that kind of money! I convinced him that all I had was twenty-five thousand. He finally agreed. I made it clear that it was the one and only time he'd get anything from me. That he'd find himself in jail, or worse, if he tried again."

Ember listened with rapt attention, her breath caught in her throat. Even with the sheriff partly blocking them, she could still feel the insanity radiating from Sean. She noticed Walker's right hand was hovering over his firearm, his left on top of the cuffs tucked into the back of the gun belt sitting on his hips.

"That Thursday night, he showed up here as I was getting ready to leave," Sean continued, his focus darting back and forth between Morton and Walker. "He tried to get another ten thousand from me. I told him no. And I meant it. I didn't think he'd follow through with his threats. He had the job at the stables, and things seemed to be going well for him. And I honestly didn't *have* that kind of extra money lying around. But that idiot had managed to spend more than he had in less than three months! He needed the cash for some sort of ridiculous down payment on a garage. A *garage!* He was threatening to ruin everything I'd worked for … over a place to park his freaking car!"

Sean's chest was heaving. Wiping at his face, he then paused for a moment and pushed two fingers against his forehead. "We fought. Tom took the first swing. At some point, we ended up in the trauma room. He was a big man and quickly got the upper hand on me. He'd thrown me against the tool tray." He took on a distant gaze, replaying the scene in his mind. "It made a huge clattering noise, and I was actually hoping at that point that someone would hear it and come help me. But then … I had the scalpel in my hand. I don't remember how it got there. And the next thing I knew, I was kneeling over Tom, and—" pausing, Sean turned his attention to Ember, as if what she thought would somehow matter. "I tried to save him. I performed CPR for … I don't know how long. But it didn't work. Nothing worked. He was dead. He was dead, and *I* killed him."

Sheriff Walker took a step toward him then, but Sean sprang back to his full height at the movement and pushed his hands out in front of him.

"Don't you see?" he begged the man that had been his friend. "It was the only way, Ben. I *had* to cover it up. It can still work," he insisted, looking at each of them in turn. "It's what's best for everyone. Morton and Sandy keep the stables, I keep my license, Vanessa gets Tom's life insurance. It was an *accident*," he emphasized again.

"You put a *knife* into a man's back." Ember's voice was unyielding. "You killed him over ten thousand dollars, Sean. You can tell yourself whatever you need to, but that's called murder, not an accident."

The tension in the room grew as Sean ignored Ember and stared at Walker, waiting to see what he would do. When his hand began to close around the grip of his pistol, Sean's eyes flicked toward the movement before meeting his friend's gaze again. Tilting his head slightly to the side, the two froze for a heartbeat.

Sean sprang into motion, throwing the door behind him open and lunging through it before Walker could draw his weapon.

"Going somewhere, doc?"

Nathan's voice was a welcome sound to Ember, and she watched with relief as he grabbed Sean around the chest and wrestled the smaller man to the floor.

TWENTY SEVEN

A storm had passed through earlier in the day, leaving in its wake the smell that can only be created by a good cleansing rain.

Ember sat on her front porch, bare feet propped up on the railing. Bands of filtered sunshine cast low in the sky danced across Crystal Lake, warming the late-summer afternoon. As she watched the sparkling water, she reflected on the parallels of the town also having its secrets washed away. Well, at least *some* of them.

"So, did you ever suspect *me*?" Mel asked from her seat beside her. "Because, if I were you, I would have totally suspected me. I've been told before that I have shifty eyes."

Laughing, Ember turned to her friend. "No, Mel. After a brief moment of uncertainty, my trust in you and your shifty eyes was unwavering."

"I don't know," Becky added from Ember's other side. "After the whole dog fiasco, I wasn't so sure."

Mel threw a sugar cookie at the older woman half-heartedly and then snorted when Becky caught it in her mouth midair. Ember relished the easy time they were able to spend together and knew better than to take any of it for granted.

Reaching for a new French press positioned on the small glass table between them, Ember topped off her cup. Mel had been right. She wasn't able to go back to drip coffee and was forever destined to be a true coffee snob.

Three days had passed since the parade and Sean's arrest. There were still some uncertainties, but the town had begun the process of putting the incident behind them.

"Do you really believe Sandy?" Mel asked in a more serious tone.

"It might seem weird, but yes," Ember answered. "You didn't see her face when I confronted her in her father's den and she first made the connection. Only, at the time, I didn't realize it. Maybe she'd suspected something all along but was unwilling to acknowledge her father would intentionally kill a horse for the money, but I don't think Morton ever told her. I believe he hid it from her."

"Still," Becky argued, "are you sure you want to work for her?"

Ember considered her aunt's words carefully. The box Morton had given her was still sitting on the kitchen table. "I consider it to be us working together rather than for her," Ember explained. "Besides, once the insurance company is done with them, there may not be much to work for. Sandy said she doesn't think her dad will do any jail time, but she's going to have to sell off a huge portion of the herd to avoid bankruptcy. It's funny," she continued, turning to look at Becky. "Sandy really isn't all that bad."

"I'll trust your judgment," Becky said, giving her a warm smile. "You've always been good at reading people."

"Apparently everyone but good-looking guys with really, really blue eyes," Mel poked.

Ember wanted to smile, but there was too much truth behind the comment. It was something that had been bothering her ever since she discovered he was the killer.

"You know, looking back, I think I always guessed there was something not quite right with him," she said, lost in thought. "But I played right into his ploy of mistrusting the easier suspects." She knew the attraction between them was real, but he used it to try and manipulate her.

"Did he really think he could make you or anyone else believe that Morton or Sandy killed Tom?" Mel asked.

Shrugging, Ember wondered the same thing. "Maybe. But I think it's more likely that he was trying to make me think they were just protecting the stables from the insurance fraud claim and was hoping I'd get scared and leave."

"He obviously doesn't know you very well," Becky replied. "And it's a good thing, too, because I don't think that lazy sheriff would have pursued things the way he did if you didn't keep pushing him! Sean was extremely close to getting away with it."

"Don't be too hard on Walker," Ember told her aunt. "He came through."

"Yeah, well, Mayor Gomez is treating you like the town hero!" Mel quipped. "Our website has two thousand likes, Ember. Two … thousand! You're a freaking celebrity!" she added, punching her lightly on her good arm.

Her other arm was in a sling. Nothing was broken, but it was badly bruised and had six stitches in it. She was determined to be using it normally by the end of the week. In spite of everything that happened, they stuck with their schedule and opened the clinic on Monday, the day before. She needed the full use of both arms in order to be as productive as she'd like.

Mel had ridden out with Becky that afternoon after the clinic closed, to help with a delivery, and Ember was happy when they agreed to stay and chat. A loud whinny rose from the fields beside the house, and Ember smiled in response. Leaning forward, she could see Daenerys and Butterscotch playing together in the arena. Earlier, Mel helped her lay fresh hay in the stables, where Butterscotch would now live.

It turned out that their behavior at the parade wasn't random. The two animals were instant best friends, and Becky's husband, Paul, was thrilled with the suggestion that Ember adopt the horse.

"What about Nathan?" Mel asked, interrupting her thoughts. "Heard anything from your knight in shining armor?"

"Like I said before, there still wasn't any armor involved," Ember pointed out, "and I'm pretty sure he was doing his job, versus trying to impress me."

"Oh, come on!" Mel insisted. "He was the first person to stop in yesterday for our grand opening."

"His dog needed its shots."

"I don't even believe it was his dog."

Laughing, Ember didn't try to deny it. "He *did* offer to take us hiking next weekend."

"*Us*?" Mel countered, her smile fading.

"Yup. It's time you experienced the great outdoors. I won't take no for an answer."

While Becky and Mel argued over the pros and cons of hiking the wilds, Ember leaned back in the seat and took it all in: the house, the lake, the laughter.

A dark blur near her arm caught her attention, and Peaches leapt into her lap. While sometimes affectionate, it was the first time he'd settled across her legs, a purr rumbling deep in his throat. As Butterscotch whinnied again in response to Daenerys's bark, a feeling Ember had been missing since she left Sanctuary swelled in her chest and made her breath catch.

The sun reached her face, and she closed her eyes, soaking in the warmth and breathing in the soft lilac scent from the fresh-cut stems on the table. A single tear trailed down her cheek and landed in the fur of her mother's cat.

I'm home.

THE END

ABOUT THE AUTHOR

Tara Meyers resides in the beautiful state of Washington. When she isn't writing, she's out hiking in the rugged Cascade Mountains, or enjoying life with her two amazing kids and several dogs! If you were entertained by this story, you might also like the novels she's written under the pen name of Tara Ellis.

Made in the USA
Lexington, KY
20 February 2019